MW00411858

"I warned you."

His arms crushed her to his bare chest as she tried to struggle upright. And then he kissed her—a kiss from an angry stranger. This was no lovemaking, for there was no love in it, no echo of the tenderness of their youth. But there was passion to spare—a passion that it humiliated her to share since all his sprang from hate.

He finally released her and lay back against the pillows, breathing hard but smiling sardonically. Joanna sat for a moment shaken and gasping for breath. Then she slapped him hard across his mocking face.

THE WIDOW OF BATH

Marian Devon

FAWCETT CREST • NEW YORK

A Fawcett Crest Book
Published by Ballantine Books
Copyright © 1982 by Marian Pope Rettke

Library of Congress Catalog Card Number: 94-94202

ISBN 0-449-21669-1

This edition published by arrangement with the Berkley/Jove Publishing Group

Manufactured in the United States of America

First Ballantine Books Edition: September 1994

10 9 8 7 6 5 4 3 2 1

Chapter One

"Joanna! Why have you never told me that you and Uncle Jack were lovers?"

Adelaide had flounced into her guardian's room and plopped down upon the foot of the Queen Anne daybed. At least the impact furnished an acceptable excuse for the jab Joanna gave her thumb. Addie surveyed the needlework apologetically. "If you make a crimson rosebud right there, the spot of blood will scarcely show at all."

"You do not feel that a single rosebud might look rather out of place in a bowl of pansies?"

Addie gave her an accusing look. "You're just trying to put me off," she said. "Tell me about you and Uncle Jack."

"You know you should not listen to servants' talk," Joanna answered, trying for a repressive tone that would put them firmly in their proper places, ward and guardian—even though the latter was only a temporary post. But as usual her attempt at authority did not work. Repressing Addie was a task for which she was ill equipped. Although Joanna usually felt like Methuselah around her husband's ebullient ward, in point of fact she was only twenty-six to Addie's seventeen, too narrow a ratio to allow for any mothering but a wide enough age span to separate their outlooks upon the world. Joanna tried again to bridge the gap.

1

"You should not encourage Emma's gossiping," she said with a frown.

Emma had been nursemaid to Joanna's husband Gerald and later to his orphaned cousins Arabella and Jack. She now performed the same duty for Toby. And she continued to view them all from a nursery perspective. There was little that ever happened that she did not know about.

"Why should I not talk to Emma? If she didn't tell me things, who would? Not you indeed! Why, compared to you the Sphinx is a prosy rattle! Uncle Jack could walk in here right now, with me never knowing that you were in love with him before your father made you marry Cousin Gerald. I need to know these things, Joanna. Heaven knows what sort of cake I might make of myself just from not realizing how the land lies. Joanna, you should have told me about the elopement the very minute you learned that Uncle Jack was coming back. Now he could be driving up to the door this very minute—" To add drama to her words, she jumped up and ran over to the window of the corner room and leaned perilously out in order to command a good view of the entrance to the house.

"For heaven's sake, do you want to freeze us both to death?" Joanna protested as a blast of cold January air hit full force, mocking the efforts of the small Adam fireplace. The sky was dull gray and threatening, providing a dismal but perhaps fitting welcome for the new heir to Welbourne Hall, one of the oldest and most rapidly decaying seats in all of Hampshire. "We don't need a sentinel, Addie. You need not worry about your uncle catching us unaware. We're bound to hear his carriage."

Addie obligingly closed the window and picked up a shawl her aunt had discarded once the fire had chased the night chill from the room. But instead of handing it to the owner, she absently draped it round her own muslin-clad shoulders.

What would Jack think of her? Joanna wondered suddenly, trying to look at Addie with a stranger's eyes—a male, related stranger's eyes at that. Why, she was a little beauty, she thought with some surprise, surveying the mass of dark shiny curls, the creamy white complexion and the huge violet eyes. Perhaps to properly fit the term, Addie needed to be a trifle taller. And her proportions at seventeen still tended to a baby plumpness, much to her distress. Still "beauty" was not far off from the mark, Joanna thought with a surge of near-maternal pride. Jack should be very proud to claim Addie for his niece. She was a stranger to him, of course. He had left two years before she and Toby had come to Welbourne Hall after their parents had drowned at sea.

"Joanna!" Addie stamped her foot and stopped her aunt's woolgathering. "Are you or are you not going to tell me about the elopement? If you don't open up right now, I vow I'll put the thumbscrews on Emma and learn every sordid detail of your poor, blighted romance."

"I thought you already had."

"Oh, no. You know what Emma is, all hints and sealed lips and 'Well, well, we know,' or 'We could, an if we would.' That's a quotation from *Hamlet*, in case you did not know," she finished smugly.

"As a matter of fact, I did. And I'm immensely gratified to learn that you profited that much from Miss Pinkerton's Academy before they felt the need to send you home."

"Joanna!"

"Very well," she sighed, putting down the picture in colored silks that she had succeeded in spoiling totally since Addie had burst into the room. "Per-

3

haps I should set the record straight before you make a Cheltenham Tragedy out of what was really just a usual juvenile episode. Your Uncle Jack and I were very close as children. I hero-worshiped him and he bear-led me shamelessly. Then when we grew older, we did plan to run away and marry. But my father found out and put a stop to it. It was a totally mad scheme, of course. We'd not have had a feather to fly with. Besides, my father was adamant that I should marry Gerald." Joanna finished up lamely under Addie's glare.

"Well, of all the Banbury stories, that one takes the cake! No, don't get up on your high ropes, Joanna. I know you aren't exactly telling me a whisker, but you are trying to fob me off with a watered-down version of what most likely really was a Cheltenham Tragedy in spite of what you say. At least Emma broke down enough to tell me that your father had Uncle Jack horsewhipped. And if that's a 'usual juvenile episode' I have yet to hear of it! Well, I can see that you aren't willing to talk about it any more than that, and since I've no wish to distress you further, I suppose I shall just have to wait and pry the story out of Uncle Jack."

"Addie, you would not!" Joanna looked so horrified that Addie hastened to reassure her.

"Don't worry. I was only funning. Of course I won't ask Uncle Jack about it. Not right away at least. But I do think it's the most romantic thing I ever heard of." She posed herself as though reading a journalistic caption. "Heir returns to claim true love and title!" she declaimed. "What a pity I can't say 'and fortune' too," she added more prosaically. "Does Uncle Jack know how deep in dun territory your Gerald left him? Good God, Joanna, whatever is the matter? You look as though you've seen a ghost."

Joanna had. The ghost of her past had truly come back to haunt her. For she had not imagined that anyone might think Jack still wished to marry her. She tried to compose herself, to look less shattered than she felt, to wonder why she'd never suspected that the servants—and the neighbors also—might so interpret Jack's return. She supposed that if one only knew of their earlier attachment and had not seen Jack's face twisted with contempt and loathing as he looked at her, or had not read his letter, so scathing that she burned it immediately but could not destroy the imprint of the bitter words that accused her of cowardice, betrayal, and title seeking, it was not so farfetched to think that they might marry. Only she knew how tragically far off the mark the gossipmongers were.

"Adelaide"—by using her proper name Joanna tried to underscore the importance of what she was trying to tell Jack's niece—"please don't couple your uncle and me in any other way than what we are: cousins-in-law." She stumbled and groped for words, trying to express the inexpressible. "Everything happened a long, long time ago and should best be forgotten. Indeed, I'm sure it is in most minds, except for those folk like Emma who live mostly in the past. I'm afraid that as the Dowager Lady Welbourne I shall be just one more in a long list of problems your uncle will be confronted with. But he won't solve that one by marrying me. So please drop that foolish notion before you make what can only be an uncomfortable homecoming an unbearable one for both of us."

She had impressed Addie, who looked at her uneasily. Not quite knowing what to say, the younger girl walked to the window and peered out again, this time contenting herself with merely pulling back the fringed curtains. "What do you suppose happened to him?" she finally asked.

It had been more than a year since Sir Gerald's death, when his cousin had become Sixth Baronet. The London solicitors had made contact as soon as a message could be carried to the Peninsula. But the Corsican was on the loose again and word had reached England that "Major Welbourne did not feel free to leave his command at just this time." Then had come the Battle of Waterloo, June 18, 1815, and the solicitor wrote again that Major Welbourne's return would be delayed once more by the necessity to convalesce from injuries received. The solicitor either did not know or would not reveal the nature of the injury. And so Joanna's mind had run the gauntlet of war horrors— blindness, disfigurement, mangled arms and legs. On and on her morbid imagination went until she resolutely clamped the lid down tight upon it.

"I don't know what his injury was," she answered Addie as if it was the first time and not the thousandth that they had speculated. "But surely it can't be too bad or someone would have warned us."

"But it's taken him six months to convalesce."

"Perhaps," Joanna answered doubtfully.

"That's so." Struck by this new thought, Addie turned to her. "Maybe he just doesn't want to come here. And who can blame him? I'm sure the solicitors must have forewarned him about how all to pieces everything around here is. And even if that weren't so, who'd want to leave the excitement of the Army for this dull place? Especially now that the fighting's over and there's the victory to celebrate. After all, he's a full-blown hero. He should be allowed to bask in all that glory for a little while." The solicitor's letter had spoken of decorations for valor in the field. "Why, I'll bet a monkey he's been playing the hero all these months and just hasn't wanted to come home. That especially makes sense now in the light of what you've just told me. For he certainly can't be anxious to see you again."

Joanna was saved from replying to this tactless observation by the noisy entrance of both their brothers. The twosome spoke together.

"I couldn't make the little wretch stick it," Godwin was saying. "Every time I asked about the principal products of Poland, I got back some form of Uncle Jack and his confounded medals." At the same time Toby exclaimed, "Nobody but a prosy wet goose would expect anyone to care a fig about Poland or its prosy principal products with Uncle Jack due home from Waterloo at any minute. It's the most famous thing that's ever happened and it's just spite on Godwin's part to go on and on about stupid old Poland the way he does. Make him stop it."

"Well, it is a rather special time for him," Joanna said lamely to her brother.

"Every day is a special day for him," Godwin glared. "And you spoil him shamelessly. You know you do. I try to cram a few facts into his head so he won't grow up a complete clod-pole, but all he has to do is run to you or Addie"— here he enlarged his glare to include Toby's older sister, who obligingly stuck her tongue out at him—"to be let do exactly as he pleases. Well, don't be amazed when you try to send him to Harrow or to Eton and they turn the little care-for-nothing down."

"The principal products of Poland will have nothing to say to that," Toby countered cheerfully. "For there's not going to be enough brass to send me there anyhow."

7

"Toby, you must not use cant phrases," Joanna murmured automatically.

"Besides," the child continued as though she had never spoken, "who wants to go to fusty old school. Just bookish slow-tops, not regular goers. I'm going to ask Uncle Jack to buy me a commission just as soon as I'm old enough and ride bravely into battle and be a hero and get a basket full of medals."

"Indeed?" Godwin retorted. "You'd better come back to the schoolroom and learn a little logic. If there's no money for school, where do you think your Uncle Jack is going to get money for a commission?"

Addie waded into the fray on behalf of her little brother. "I'll buy it for him when I come of age. Or he can wait till he's reached his own majority and buy it for himself. But for heaven's sake, will you two leave off wrangling? We don't want Uncle Jack to walk in and find you at daggers drawn. You're supposed to be Toby's mentor, Godwin." She said the word quite proudly and the tutor's eyebrows went up that she should know it. "But instead you squabble like an eight-year-old yourself."

She had a point. In theory it had seemed a solution to two problems to have Joanna's nineteen-year-old brother serve as Toby's tutor. Godwin was, in one way, well equipped to do so. He was the family intellectual, bookish almost to a fault. But after their father's death, he'd had to interrupt his Cambridge studies from lack of funds. And since Sir Gerald Welbourne had left his affairs in such a jumble, his widow had not felt free to hire a governess for Toby. So to have Godwin close Blackthorn Hall and take on Toby's education while his own bailiff strove to salvage an estate left heavily encumbered had seemed at first a master stroke of management on Joanna's part. But Godwin and

Toby were oil and water. Godwin was a poet—with a poet's soul, as he forever told them—which meant that when he was not actually engaged in reading or in writing verse, he was gazing off into middle distance looking pensive or tortured. Lord Byron was his hero. And it was his cross to be fair-haired and rather ordinary looking instead of romantically dark and Greek-god handsome like the poet who had dazzled both the critics and the country four years before with *Childe Harold's Pilgrimage*.

Toby, on the other hand, was everything that his tutor least appreciated—perpetual energy, a lover of sport of any kind but especially those pursuits involving horses, and a hero-worshiper of anyone who participated in England's great victories on the Continent. He had brown eyes and hair, a roundish face, and an engaging smile, enhanced not hampered by a missing tooth. His disposition was usually sunny, but occasionally it was subject to storms that burst suddenly and terribly, though briefly, over all their heads.

"Oh, I say, Joanna." Toby jumped up from the daybed where he'd squeezed in between Addie and his aunt and began to gallop like a horse in his excitement. "Do you suppose that Uncle Jack will allow me to ride Champion and take me fox hunting with him?"

"Undoubtedly," his tutor sneered. "There never was a Welbourne worthy of the name who wouldn't drop any sort of pursuit imaginable to follow a pack of hounds with a pack of men of the same mentality and ride down and execute a little fox that never did any harm to anybody, except a few stupid chickens here and there."

Both Toby and Addie bristled. They might be Welbournes only on their mother's side, but Godwin's words were a sacrilege in their eyes.

9

"Killing the fox is not the point and you know it perfectly well!" Addie raced in ahead of Toby to exclaim. "If you didn't have such a stupid attitude toward horses, you'd know it is the thrill of the riding that counts."

"Oh? Then why not omit the fox from the dramatis personae altogether?" Godwin countered. Before Addie could reply, Toby pulled his own guns into position and let go a salvo.

"Just because you don't happen to like it is no reason to think that hunting is odious. Anything you don't happen to know how to do is always odious. If you had your way, the whole world would just sit around and write poems to one another." And he proceeded to strike a pose that the great Kean himself might well have envied. "To an Uncaring Nymph," Toby declaimed, placing his hands upon his heart. "By Godwin Carrothers.

"Uncaring Nymph—when I cast aside
This mortal robe and lay me down to rest,
Come! See 'The False Felicia'
Emblazoned upon my breast."

"You little beast!" The tutor's face had grown livid.

"The False Felicia!" Addie, insensitive as always to Godwin's finer feelings, convulsed into whoops, and Joanna was hard put not to join in. Perhaps the only thing that saved her was the need to intervene if Godwin decided to strangle Toby.

"Oh, I say, Godwin." Toby suddenly abandoned his theatrical pose and looked quite troubled. "Do you really intend for them to lay you out starkers when you die? I should hate it above all things. I mean it's bad enough to be dead without a fellow

10

having to take off all his clothes and lie there starkers with people standing around reading messages he'd written on himself. I mean, why don't you just leave her a note instead?"

Joanna did laugh then. Though not quite as uncontrollably as Addie, who at that point was rolling on the floor. That fact probably saved Toby's life, for Godwin hesitated a moment deciding which one to make his first victim. But then over all the noisy mirth they heard the sound of carriage wheels. All noise and action froze. Toby raced to the window and flung it open.

"Hurrah!" he shouted. "He's here! Uncle Jack is here!"

Chapter Two

ADDIE DASHED AFTER Toby and leaned out, grabbing him firmly by his short jacket. Even Godwin forgot his injured dignity and ran to the window in time to see a smart-looking curricle, closely followed by a larger carriage, sweeping round the curving drive. In case the curricle driver glanced up to see them gawking there, Joanna used her brother as a shield, but none of the other three stared any harder.

"What a bang-up rig," little Toby breathed, drawing Joanna's attention momentarily to the shiny brand-newness of the curricle with its bright red upholstery and wheels and to the high-stepping pair that pulled it, matched so perfectly in size and color as to give the illusion of seeing double. But immediately its driver reclaimed her gaze and she felt her knees begin to tremble and her mouth go dry. If an aerial view of the top of a curly brimmed beaver could have this effect, she wondered, how on earth would she be able to confront him?

"He can't have been hurt too badly," Addie said excitedly, drawing her head back. "Or he could not have driven himself all the way from London."

"Thank God," Joanna breathed, but the words stuck somewhere in her constricted throat.

Servants were suddenly appearing. Obviously they, too, had been lurking near the windows awaiting the arrival. Two grooms materialized to take hold of the horses' bridals while Banks the butler descended the front steps, his almost regal dignity for once forgotten in a beaming smile. He was closely followed by a footman who, with the help of the military-looking servant who had climbed down from the chaise, took charge of the luggage the veteran had brought.

"Welcome home, Sir John." For all their obvious sincerity, the butler's words rang falsely to Joanna's ears. "Sir John." Sir John was some stranger who had just arrived. Not "Coppy," whom she'd grown up with and idolized. Not even "Jack."

"Thank you, Banks. You're looking fit." The voice was coolly formal. Joanna edged back from the window. Though the beaver had not tilted up their way, she somehow concluded that Sir John Welbourne was conscious of his audience.

"Why, he's wearing trowsers!" It was hard to tell if Godwin was impressed or shocked as he watched Jack climb down from his curricle. Sure enough, instead of the snugly fitting breeches inside boots usually affected by English country gentlemen, he was wearing the looser trowsers just coming into fashion on the Continent, inspired, they said, by the upsurge of French democracy.

"I say, he's a regular Corinthian," Addie reported admiringly. The others agreed, either silently or otherwise, as they gawked down at the perfectly tailored greatcoat with its several capes, which Joanna realized required no padding over the broad shoulders. It lay open to allow a glimpse of snowy shirt points, high enough to be fashionable but not uncomfortable as they rose above the neckerchief draped artfully at his throat. The trowsers were biscuit colored and the boots that peeped out from underneath them gleamed as brightly as any

13

tasseled Hessians sported for display. Even his civilian clothes looked military, Joanna thought as Jack stood chatting for a moment with the butler. Toby must have been thinking along those lines too for he spoke up suddenly. "Why didn't he wear his uniform? I most particularly desired to see it."

"Because he's a civilian now," Godwin retorted. "A fine cake he'd make of himself parading around in fancy dress after everyone knows he's sold out of the Army."

"I don't care," Toby answered stubbornly. "It's still his. And he could wear it if he wanted to. Only maybe," he cheered up immensely, "it got spoiled at Waterloo. Do you suppose it has bulletholes all through it? Or even saber cuts?" Joanna shuddered at such a grizzly thought, but Toby was obviously transported by the possibility.

Jack Welbourne moved toward the door then and his observers simultaneously observed the limp. Godwin, Toby, and Addie remarked at once.

"Look, it's his leg that was injured."

"He's limping."

"It can't be too bad. It's hardly noticeable."

The last was true. As Sir John walked toward the front entrance, the limp was very slight. But again Joanna had the impression that he was using all his willpower to keep it so as he passed underneath their gaze.

Addie's voice rang with relief. "Thank God. I was afraid something dreadful might have happened to him. But a slight limp's not bad at all. Just makes him seem distinguished."

"That's true," Godwin chimed in. "Why, even Byron has a limp."

Joanna managed a murmur of agreement for she did share their sentiments a thousandfold. But even so, she could not dismiss Jack's disability as

14

lightly as they seemed to. For she knew how he would hate it. Physical perfection was important to him. Even as a lad he'd had to run faster, jump further, and climb higher than anybody else did. Being crippled, even slightly so, would be a cross for him to bear, no matter how Byronic or romantic it might appear to others.

"Let's go! Huzzah! He's really here!" Toby shrieked and ran out of the room with Godwin calling after him, "Slow down, you little horror! Don't act like such a widgeon!"

Addie was almost as excited as her little brother. "Come on." She grabbed Joanna by the hand. "We must welcome my uncle back to Welbourne Hall. Isn't this the most fabulous thing? I can tell already that I admire him prodigiously."

"How can you tell that from a hat crown?" Godwin asked witheringly.

But for once Addie chose to ignore his bait and gave Joanna's hand a tug. "Come on, hurry. It will look uncivil for no one to be at the door but Toby."

"No. I cannot." The words came tumbling out, betraying Joanna's sudden panic.

Addie turned toward her in astonishment.

"I'm sorry. I've only just remembered. I must go see Mrs. Crocker right away and take some things I promised."

The excuse sounded contrived, even to Joanna. She realized that it would be boorish beyond belief not to greet her husband's heir. As mistress of the house, no matter how temporarily, it was, she knew, her place to do so. But she could not face him. Not just then. Not till she was calmer. Jack would understand, for it would not be her first time to funk a crisis. But Addie was shocked by her behavior. Even Godwin was looking oddly at his sister.

15

"But—" Addie started to protest, then something she saw in Joanna's face made her change her mind. "Very well, then. I'll tell Uncle Jack that you were called away quite urgently, that Mrs. Crocker is hovering on the brink. Though if he remembers her, he'll know that she's been 'hovering' for these twenty years or more." Mrs. Crocker was their bailiff's ancient mother and tyrannized him and all his household with her illnesses. "Well, you come on, Godwin, anyhow."

He merely shrugged. "I'm only the tutor here, if you recall. It would be most inappropriate for me to welcome the warrior home."

"Good God!" Addie expostulated, disgusted with the pair of them. "What a time for both you Carrothers to get into a taking." And she went flouncing off to hail the conquering hero by herself.

Godwin looked at his sister with something akin to sympathy. Joanna wondered suddenly how well he remembered Jack and how much he knew of their past history. He had, after all, been twelve years old when Jack had gone away. And certainly Godwin possessed a poet's sensibility, if perhaps not quite a poet's talent. Now all he said was, "You'd better get your soup or calf's-foot jelly or whatever and be off with it if you don't wish to meet the hero face-to-face in spite of all. For I wouldn't put it past that little monster Toby to throw a rub in your way by bringing his Uncle Jack straight up here to you."

"He wouldn't come," Joanna answered. But just the same she took no chances. Snatching her shawl from where Addie had abandoned it, she headed down the back stairs toward the kitchen. Five minutes later, wearing pattens and a heavy cloak that Cook had insisted on, Joanna headed down the lane that would lead her to a narrow footpath.

16

Already she regretted her decision. The lane was a mass of mud from a prolonged wet season. The wind rattled the few remaining dried-up leaves upon the trees that flanked the lane and chilled straight to the bone. The slate-colored sky pressed earthward, as downcast as her mood. Then, to add the final note of misery, it began to rain again, a sniveling sort of rain that went almost imperceptibly from mist to tearlike drops streaming down Joanna's face.

Behind her she heard the sound of carriage wheels and thought that being splashed with mud would be the final straw. She gathered up her bedraggled skirts and prepared to leap the ditch well out of splatter range. But the coachman gruffly coaxed his horses to a halt and a familiar voice called out, "Joanna Welbourne! Why on earth are you out walking in such weather? You'll catch your death!" Joanna stopped her leap to turn and see her favorite neighbor and dear friend, Miss Harriet Newcomb, leaning out her carriage window. "Get in here at once, child," she said imperiously, "and I'll have William drive you wherever it is you have to go."

Joanna almost made an excuse about needing exercise, for she wasn't up to facing even a good friend. Miss Newcomb had been her mother's closest confidante, and after that lady's untimely death she had become, if not quite a mother to Joanna, at least a treasured aunt.

As soon as Joanna had settled into the coach, spraying water like a wet dog in the process, Miss Newcomb exercised some of the forthrightness she was famous for. Her shrewd look took in the young woman's unhappy face as well as the sodden basket she was carrying. "Well, I had heard that Mrs. Crocker has had another of her famous sinking

17

spells. But just the same, the only possible reason I can think of for you to be tramping down the lane in such a downpour is that Jack Welbourne has come home and you're in full flight from him. Tell me if I'm wrong."

"You aren't wrong that Jack is home," Joanna answered stiffly.

"And I'm not wrong about the other either. Now don't get on your high ropes with me. I've known you for too long now to stand on points with you. I can take it, then, that he has not forgiven you?"

"I don't know."

"What do you mean, you do not know? How did he behave toward you? Brotherly or at daggers drawn or somewhere in between perhaps?" When Joanna did not answer right away, Miss Newcomb reached over and patted her bare hand, then dried her own kid glove carefully so it would not spot. "Joanna, if you do not get a putrid fever from trudging around in this weather, not even wearing gloves to protect your skin, I shall be astonished. But never mind what I just said. I'm a prying, meddlesome woman and I shall now try minding my own business for a change."

They rode in silence for a bit, Joanna locked in misery while her friend studied her covertly. "I'm out making morning calls," Miss Newcomb finally remarked. "Partly because I wish to, and partly," she smiled to take any sting out of the observation, "to escape my niece Felicia. I don't believe you've met my niece as yet."

"No. But Godwin most certainly has had that pleasure." Joanna was able to smile back then as Miss Newcomb's expressive eyes danced at the mention of her brother.

"Oh, yes. He has been invaluable. In London Felicia was, I gather, rather in the position of Alexan-

18

der the Great, except that whereas he had no more worlds left to conquer, she had no remaining hearts to break. Not that that was the entire reason for her coming here." Miss Newcomb could not quite hide the disapproval underneath her twinkle. "Felicia is quite a headstrong girl and manages too often, I'm afraid, to lose sight of what is proper conduct for a gently bred young lady. Nothing terribly wicked, you understand," she hastily explained, "but certainly her behavior often tends to be ill advised, if not actually scandalous. At any rate, after her latest escapade her father, my younger brother, you may recall, decided she should rusticate a bit and sent her down to me. She is quite an heiress, you understand, and very pretty. But even so, her hoydenish behavior could prevent the brilliant sort of match they are hoping she will make. They wish to give Society an opportunity to forget her latest start."

Joanna gave an exaggerated sigh. "Poor Godwin. What bad luck to be smitten by someone so far above his touch. No one could possibly term him a good match."

Miss Newcomb did not try to contradict her, which spoke volumes for her brother's chances, but resumed a bantering tone. "Oh, but just think, Joanna, how awful it would be if she did not break his heart. He is, after all, a poet. We must not lose sight of that. And genius feeds on misery."

"Yes, indeed. The 'False Felicia.'"

"You've read his latest then? It is, I fear, the sequel to the 'Fair Felicia.'"

They were approaching the Crocker cottage. Miss Newcomb offered to have William wait while Joanna delivered her delicacies and then drive her home, but she declined. "No, truly. The rain has slacked off again. And I really need the exercise."

"Well, do not allow Mrs. Crocker to keep you sitting in those damp clothes while she recites her ills. And change them as soon as you get home," Miss Newcomb chided, sounding very much like Joanna's mother. "And, Joanna," she waved William still again as he clucked up the horses, "I shall soon be sending a note around. I want all of you to take family supper with us. Felicia needs the society of young people and I am, of course, most desirous of seeing Jack again. I shall give him a day or so to settle in, then you all must come to Fairview."

After spending half an hour with Mrs. Crocker, Joanna had ample time, while trudging back down the muddy lane, to regret her rashness in bolting from the house the minute Jack arrived. She was growing painfully aware that by taking flight she'd made a bad matter far, far worse. Typical, she thought bitterly. She'd never been able to face up to things squarely the way she should. Instead she felt herself far too prone to skirt around an issue or postpone it, a tactic that often magnified the problem instead of easing it. "Get back on immediately," Jack had insisted when her horse had thrown her when she was small. And always she'd done exactly what he said. Now she had no fear of horses, but she'd never been able to apply the same principle to other areas of her life. She should have, she now believed, faced Jack Welbourne immediately with all naturalness as the Dowager Lady Welbourne. Instead, by running away, she'd announced to everyone, especially to her husband's heir, that she was afraid to face him—circumstantial evidence, he'd believe, of a guilt she'd long denied. Joanna was not at all in charity with herself as she entered Welbourne Hall by a side door seldom used.

Addie, Toby, and Godwin were all there in her room, seated on the floor before the hearth. Toby went immediately on the attack. "Really, Joanna. I say, it's not at all the thing! You should have been here to do the polite when Uncle Jack arrived. He must have thought it quite odd of you."

"Do be quiet, Toby." Addie rushed to their aunt's defense. "Imagine you reading anyone, especially Joanna, a lecture upon good manners!"

But Toby was primed with righteous indignation. "I don't care what you think, it was not at all the thing. Was it the thing, Joanna?"

"Perhaps not," Joanna answered while she hung her dripping cloak beside the fire to dry, then sat down on the floor beside them. "But I had promised to visit Mrs. Crocker. And besides, I thought your uncle would like to see you and Addie first. He and I are not actually related, you know, except by marriage."

As an excuse, this sounded rather lame, but Toby brightened up. "That's so. I expect he was most eager to see me—and Addie too, although she's just a girl. For it's true that you are only the wife—that is, the widow—of his cousin."

"You sound like a French phrase book," his tutor snorted, but Toby ignored the interruption and went on.

"And he probably didn't like Uncle Gerald above half. Nobody else did at any rate."

"Toby!" There was real distress in Joanna's voice as she reproved him.

"Well, you did, I suppose," he amended tactfully. "But then you had to, I expect. For you were married to him. But I certainly didn't like him above half myself. Did you like him, Godwin?"

"No," Joanna's brother answered briefly.

"Well, just the same, you should not speak ill of the dead," Addie interposed.

"Whyever not?" Toby bristled. "Just because a

21

person's dead is no reason to tell a bunch of whiskers. You didn't like Uncle Gerald either. And the servants didn't either. Not even Emma. She said once that he was a horrid little boy. So there. Nobody liked him, except Joanna of course because she had to, so I bet a monkey Uncle Jack didn't like him either. He couldn't have. Uncle Gerald was a complete loose screw while Uncle Jack is up to snuff. You can tell right off."

Godwin gave a derisive snort, but Adelaide made a duet of her brother's hymn of praise. "Oh, he is, Joanna. You should have told me that Uncle Jack is so utterly and devastatingly good-looking. And he possesses such an air. His face is so—so—masklike that I'm sure he must be hiding a broken heart behind his brave exterior."

"Fustian!" said Godwin. "He was probably just bone-tired from traveling and had a touch of dyspepsia besides from watching you and Toby make cakes of yourselves over him. Of all the toadeaters that I ever overheard. Ow!" Here Godwin clutched his leg where Toby had just kicked him.

"Toby!" Joanna scolded. "You absolutely must curb your odious habit of kicking people on the shins. How many times have I—"

"Well, I don't blame Toby!" Addie glared at Godwin. "Toadeaters indeed! We were only trying to be very cordial to make up for your and Joanna's shabby behavior. And he is a real, genuine hero after all. And I do admire him prodigiously. In fact, I think I shall quite end up by falling in love with him."

"Don't be absurd," Godwin countered. "You can't, for he's your uncle."

"What has that to say anything? If your precious Byron can have an affair with his half sister, then what's to prevent me from—"

22

"That's a lie and a damned one at that!" Godwin leaped to his feet, his face red and his fists clinched at this slander of his hero. "How you can even repeat such vile filth is more than I can understand. It's a pack of lies—circulated by Philistines who can never hope to understand the higher feelings of a man of genius. They can't begin to know—"

"And I suppose you can? I'm sure that Lord Byron keeps you well informed on all of his affairs!" Addie jumped up too and they stood toe to toe spitting at one another like two wet cats while Toby edged closer to them on the floor and tugged at his sister's skirt.

"Go it, Addie!" he egged her on.

Joanna wanted nothing so much as to clear the lot of them and their squabblings out of her room, but she felt powerless to do so. Her head was beginning to ache dully, and she recalled Miss Newcomb's warning about a putrid fever. And then, like the crack of doom, a knock came at the door. "Come in," she called above Godwin and Addie's bickering. Annie the maid poked her head inside.

"He's asking for you, miss." In her excitement Annie could not be bothered with modes of proper address. But then, misinterpreting Joanna's frozen look, she backed up and tried again. "Sir John would like to see Lady Welbourne in the library at her earliest convenience. What shall I tell him?"

"You need not tell him anything," Joanna answered. "I'll go down right away."

Chapter Three

THE LIBRARY DOOR had been left ajar, giving Joanna a moment to watch Jack unobserved. He sat at the desk, a decanter at his elbow and a stack of estate books piled up before him. He had changed, she thought, then chided herself for being startled by something that inevitable. Of course he had changed. What didn't change in seven years? And to time must be added the bitterness of his leaving and all those years of war.

Even so, it was not his physical appearance that she found so altered. True, his hair had turned from its boyish brilliance to a darker, unburnished hue and was now cut and swept into the modern Brutus style. The bones of his face were a bit more prominent, the skin stretched tightly, with little lines of bitterness—or pain, perhaps—around the eyes and mouth. But still physically he was not all that different from the boy she'd grown up with. The change was really indefinable. But Joanna knew that this man was a stranger. "Coppy" was gone for good and was never coming back.

He glanced up suddenly to see her watching, and for an instant she thought it was going to be all right. Then the dark eyes hardened while the stern mouth went through the motions of a smile. "Come in, Joanna, and close the door behind you."

Jack's eyes never left her face as she walked to-

24

ward him. Instead of getting to his feet, he tilted his own chair backward and gestured toward a small gilded one already pulled up before the massive desk. She sat down upon it, feeling for all the world like a little girl called on the carpet for some childish misdemeanor. Then she reminded herself of her twenty-six years and widow's status and raised her head to look Jack squarely in the eye. The smile increased. So did its chilliness.

"Well, well. The even more beautiful Miss Joanna Carrothers. Your father must be whirling in his grave. But then he always was a slow-top, was he not? Now it appears that, true to form, he backed the wrong matrimonial horse for you. But possibly that's not fair. Who knows—if you had married me, perhaps Gerald might not have met such an untimely end."

It was odd, Joanna thought, that his words failed to wound her the way he meant them to. But this stranger seemed to lack the power to hurt. She sat looking at him—staring actually—trying to bring some sort of reconciliation between her memories and this reality.

"Well," he mocked, "I see you do not choose to take my bait. But then you always did loathe scenes of any sort. Or, surely, you have not been struck dumb during these past seven years and no one thought to mention it?"

"No, of course not," she found her tongue at last and blurted out. "It's just that I was startled. I'd never thought before that you and Gerald looked anything alike."

The mocking guard was down now and his face turned a dull red, almost the color of his hair. "By God, I hope not," he answered viciously. "Perhaps you're led astray by the decanter here. I understand that Gerald was never without one. The result, no doubt, of his happy marriage."

"No, it was not that at all." Joanna had somehow become more calm, now that Jack's control was shattered. "I think it was some trick of expression that reminded me of Gerald for an instant. You never used to sneer."

"I never used to have the cause. But I hope you slander me unnecessarily. Perhaps your conscience drives you to see your husband everywhere. I see that you're still wearing the willow for him." He gestured toward Joanna's gown. "Tell me, don't you think all that black a bit excessive—given both the circumstances of your marriage and those of Gerald's death? It's been well over a year now. I find it difficult to believe that you're still repining his loss."

"I'm wearing black," Joanna replied with dignity, "because my mourning clothes are all I have that are even slightly close to being in the current mode." She nodded toward the ledgers. "You've been appraised of our finances. I hardly wanted to put us even further into debt by ordering a new wardrobe."

"How excessively noble of you," he murmured. "And here I'd been thinking uncharitably that you were wearing black because it contrasts so dramatically with your fair hair."

"Did you only ask me here to give me a setdown?" Joanna could not quite keep her voice from trembling. "No doubt you deserve the opportunity, but I can't see that after all these years much purpose can be served by it. As you yourself have just pointed out, you now have most of what you always coveted. And as for me, you also seem aware that I brought no happiness to Gerald. So can you not

26

consider yourself fortunate on all counts? I see no need for us to be at daggers drawn."

"You're right," he replied, but with no softening in his face or voice. "That's really why I sent for you. I wished to put us on some sort of footing we could live with." Joanna's brows shot up but he ignored that and went on. "From the feeble excuses for your departure that my nephew and niece kept making up, I got the distinct impression you were avoiding me. No matter how we both might wish for that, it's hardly possible. So I thought we might do better to have our initial meeting away from curious eyes. But once again I find myself mistaken in you. We would undoubtedly have done better with an audience."

"No, you were right, of course. We do need a private moment to come to terms with a situation that must be very distasteful to you. I have given it much thought since Gerald's death, and the most sensible solution is for me to remove to the Dower House. So with your permission I'll do it right away."

"No."

"I beg your pardon?"

"No. That will be impossible. You've just said yourself that Gerald left the estates in a damnable mess. Face facts for once, Joanna. If you realize that I can't afford a new wardrobe for you, just how the devil do you think I can stand the expense of two establishments? No, I'm afraid we shall all have to accommodate ourselves, temporarily at any rate, here at Welbourne Hall. Besides, you weren't thinking of abandoning Addie and Toby, were you? Is that not rather unfeeling on your part?"

"I had thought to take them with me," she answered stiffly.

"I'm afraid it's hardly practical. If you'd bothered

27

to go through the Dower House, you'd know that. According to Crocker, it's uninhabitable. I suppose I could accommodate myself well enough among the damp rot and the falling plaster. After all, I'm accustomed to bivouacking in the open. But if I did move, or for that matter if the rest of you removed yourselves, I think we'd find ourselves the subject of more gossip in the neighborhood than we'd care to. No, Joanna, I think we'll have to manage somehow to rub along together."

"Very well then." Joanna rose slowly to her feet. Instead of paying her the courtesy of standing up or seeing her out as she walked away, Jack turned his attention to the ledgers once again. The interview had undoubtedly been a failure from both their points of view, Joanna thought. They'd certainly not arrived at "some sort of footing" they could live with. She hesitated with her hand upon the doorknob, feeling compelled to try again for a better understanding, to recall to him those times when they were merely friends, those childhood days before he'd come down from Oxford to glance across a ballroom and see her all grown up and had fallen in love with her. She took a deep breath and forced herself to turn once more and face him. But whatever words she might have spoken were swept away by the look of suffering on his face.

"Coppy—" In her concern Joanna took a step toward him but was halted in her tracks as his pain swiftly turned to fury.

"Don't call me that." His voice was low but shook with rage. "We're rather old, do you not agree, for nursery names. People who know me well call me Jack."

"Then perhaps I should call you John." She could be just as bitter as he, Joanna was discovering.

28

"For it's evident that I do not know you any more at all."

"Or better still, Sir John," he snarled back. "Since you're so fond of titles—even a jumped-up one belonging to a down-at-the-heels baronetcy. But never mind all that. What did you start to say?"

"Nothing of the slightest importance, Sir John," Joanna answered and went out. She spent the rest of the afternoon regretting everything she'd said and shoring herself up for their next encounter.

Dinner was a disaster. In fact, in retrospect it would not have surprised Joanna much to learn that the hero of Waterloo preferred the battle to the first day of his homecoming. The Welbournes kept country hours and dined at five. Cook had outdone herself with the menu Joanna had given her, especially with the scrag of veal and the Hessian ragout, old favorites with Jack. But like everything else about him, his taste in food had changed, Joanna realized, as she watched him push Cook's masterpieces about his plate, eating very little. The lines of strain were etched even deeper in his face, making her wonder once again if he suffered pain. Most likely, she concluded, the distress was of a mental sort and came from being saddled with all the problems involved with his inheritance, including her unwanted presence in Welbourne Hall.

Except for Toby, all the family seemed to share the strain. Godwin had greeted Jack with near hostility, more from jealousy Joanna suspected than from loyalty to her. For in spite of his constant protestations otherwise, she knew that Godwin secretly envied the type of man her cousin-in-law seemed to be, the sportsman-soldier who moved among his peers with self-assured manliness. His mere presence served to make Godwin revert to awkward adolescence.

Addie, too, was subdued and quiet. Joanna deeply regretted that the girl had heard all the gossip about things past. Normally Addie could have been counted on to at least distract, if not absolutely charm, her uncle.

As it was, the whole burden of conversation rested upon Toby's shoulders. At first he was unaware of the undercurrents. He had begun pelting Jack with questions the moment the soldier entered the blue saloon, where the family had gathered to await Banks's call to dinner, and the catechism had continued on the way into the dining chamber. Initially Jack appeared to welcome the distraction, for it almost obscured the fact that he was limping rather badly, certainly more so than upon his entrance to the house. Why doesn't he use a cane, Joanna thought irritably. How stupid and typical to be determined not to give in to weakness.

But later at the table, by the time of the first remove, Jack's answers to Toby's questions, which had never been expansive, became quite terse.

"What was it like on the Peninsula?"

"Hot and dirty."

"Did you ever actually see Napoleon?"

"Yes, through a spy glass."

"Oh, famous! What was he doing?"

"Looking back at us."

"Did you know the Duke of Wellington?"

"Yes."

"Personally, I mean."

"Yes, I did."

Here Godwin could stand the strain no longer and growled in Toby's ear, "Hush up, brat, and let him eat," causing Addie to hiss at him, "Who do you think you are, speaking to my little brother in that fashion?" to which Godwin hissed back, "His tutor, for my sins!"

In desperation Joanna turned to Jack. "I saw Miss Newcomb today and she sends her best regards. She said to tell you she will be calling soon."

"Oh, was she also on your Ministering Angel list? I'd understood you'd gone to see the ailing Mrs. Crocker. Is Miss Newcomb ill as well? You really do seem to play the Lady Bountiful." There was no attempt to cloak his hostility. Jack sat at the head of the table and Joanna at the foot and the three young people stared at his mocking face and at her stricken one. Addie and Godwin looked shocked and uncomfortable. Toby looked astounded.

"Uncle Jack," he blurted out, "aren't you going to marry Joanna?"

A mortar shell exploding in the table centerpiece would have been less devastating. They all sat stunned. The candlelight began to swim and Joanna briefly closed her eyes. When she opened them again, Jack's gaze had left her face and was riveted to Toby's. "Good God, no," he said. "Where did you ever get such a ramshackle idea?"

Now even Toby could not miss the venom in his uncle's tone. His lower lip began to quiver, but he got himself manfully under quick control and glared back at Jack, suddenly looking all Welbourne. "Emma said you'd most likely marry Joanna now since you wanted to once but her papa wouldn't let you."

"Emma quite mistakes the matter."

"Toby, do be quiet," Addie commanded, but there was no stopping her little brother. Like a true knight errant, he went on the attack, though Joanna could see he was bewildered by the necessity to defend her.

"I don't think it's a ramshackle idea at all, marrying Joanna, I mean to say. And if you don't wish to,

31

well then when I come of age and get my fortune I'll marry her myself."

"That sounds like the type of solution to her difficulties that most appeals to Lady Welbourne. Just how large is your fortune, Toby?"

"Damn your impudence," Godwin muttered but hadn't quite the courage to say it louder. Jack either did not hear or chose to ignore him. Joanna was too stricken to say anything. It fell to Addie to try desperately to restore some sense of normalcy to the shattered family dinner.

She switched the subject. "Uncle Jack, have you seen the stables yet?"

"No, I haven't. Are they as run-down as everything else around here?" Jack forced a smile as he asked the question, regretting, Joanna felt sure, his lapse into boorishness.

"Of course not," Godwin snarled. "I'm surprised that you should even ask. Your cousin took good care of them in true Welbourne style. A Welbourne might let his ancestral seat go to rack and ruin, his lands lie fallow, his tenants starve, his children go uneducated, but you can rest assured that until the sheriff drags the last one off for debts, the Welbournes will see to it that their horses are treated like four-footed kings."

Surprisingly Jack grinned at that, acknowledging the hit. But Toby, who recognized an insult when he heard it, felt called upon to take away the sting. "Godwin just feels that way because he doesn't ride. Not ever."

"Oh," Jack said, making an obvious effort to be civil. "If the stables are as well stocked as you imply, there should be some cattle there to suit you. Don't hesitate to use them any time you like."

"He doesn't ride because he can't," Toby piped up

32

once more. Godwin's face turned red. "He doesn't even know how to ride a horse."

Jack couldn't quite wipe the incredulity from his face in time for Godwin not to see it, but he kept it from his voice. "I'll be happy to teach you myself," he said politely, "any time you like."

"Like hell you will!" Godwin exploded, springing to his feet, sending his chair crashing to the floor. "I'll see you damned first!" And with that he flung himself from the dining room, slamming the door behind him.

The rest of the party sat transfixed, except for Toby who simply confiscated Godwin's untouched sweet and began to eat it. The clatter of his spoon was the only sound for minutes. Then Jack addressed the room in general. "Just what the devil was that in aid of? I thought I was trying to do the lad a favor."

"Well, you weren't," Toby answered, his mouth crammed full of trifle. "You'd have done better to ask him to play with snakes. Godwin hates horses. He's afraid of them. In fact, Godwin's something of a coward. Comes of being a poet, I expect."

"He is not a coward, you little monster!" Now it was Addie's turn to blaze. "What do you know about it anyhow? It took a lot more courage to stand up to Uncle Gerald and take all his beatings than it does to ride a st-stupid horse—which any peagoose, including you, can do." And with that she too jumped up and ran from the dining room.

"Well, you've just liberated one more pudding, Toby," Jack said dryly. "Tell me, does this family always leave the table so dramatically?"

"No." Toby reached out for Addie's untouched sweet. Joanna knew that she should stop him, but at the moment she was more than willing for him to have a stomachache.

"Then can you explain that scene to me, Joanna?" Jack reached for the port and filled his glass. "What did Adelaide mean about Gerald beating Godwin?"

"Right after we were married," her voice stumbled at the term, "Gerald decided that Godwin must learn to ride and undertook to teach him. Godwin was bookish, you remember, and not into sport. And Gerald was ashamed to have a brother, even by marriage, who wasn't as at home in the saddle as in a chair. In Godwin's defense, I think the horse Gerald provided was quite unsuitable for a novice of his size. At any rate, he fell off and refused to get back up again. And Gerald thrashed him. After that, there was a series of 'riding lessons'"—she twisted the words bitterly—"when Gerald dragged Godwin to the stables, then beat him when he refused to mount. Godwin proved even more stubborn, however, than your cousin. Gerald finally had to abandon the idea. But Godwin had no love of horses and has refused ever since to ride."

"Good God! No wonder. Couldn't you have stopped it?" he asked and then his face twisted with contempt. "No, I don't suppose you could have." He picked up his glass and studied the ruby contents for a moment. "Well, Toby, you told me earlier that your ambition is to be a soldier. Allow me to recommend the life. I think you'll find it much, much simpler than domestic bliss." He lifted his glass to his lips and his eyes mocked Joanna across the rim. "God bless England and our happy home." He drank deeply as she took Toby by the hand and they left him to his port.

34

Chapter Four

"JOANNA! YOU SIMPLY must take that ninnyhammer in charge—or God knows what will happen."

Godwin stood glaring down at his sister, breathing righteous indignation. After a near-sleepless night, Joanna had stayed late in bed. Now she hoped that the extra rest plus several cups of tea would rid her of the dull ache behind her eyes. But it was not to be.

"Which ninnyhammer?" she asked him. But the question was rhetorical, a way of staving off the crisis through an extra sip or two. For she knew the answer. Toby might exasperate her brother till he longed to throttle him, but only Addie could send him flying up into the boughs where he was now.

Their relationship was a bit unusual, to say the least, more like brother and sister than Joanna and he with their age difference could ever be. Though they were constantly bickering, Joanna felt sure, or hoped at any rate, that they held each other in true affection. Right now underneath all his bombast she could sense Godwin's real concern.

"It's Addie, Joanna. You've simply got to do something before she gets herself into the kind of scrape that even the prospects of her famous fortune won't be able to make right for her."

"Oh, really, Godwin. Don't look so Friday-faced.

It's too early in the morning for any crisis. Besides, Addie doesn't want entirely for sense, you know."

"You think not?" her brother retorted bitterly. "Then explain to me what a girl of sense was doing kissing a groom?"

"Good God!"

"Exactly. I was out for a stroll and I spotted their two horses turned loose to wander off to China if they wished to, but luckily the beasts were content to stay grazing by the hedgerow. So I peeped over to see what was going on. I thought the little hoyden might have been thrown—and more's the pity that she wasn't, right on her empty head—but there they were, kneeling down so as not to be seen from the lane and Addie was kissing that clod for all she was worth."

"Bert?"

"Of course Bert. Who did you think, Old Peterson?"

The image of young Bert floated before Joanna's eyes, all muscles and black hair—and virility. The very type to make a bored, impressionable girl like Addie lose all sense of propriety and fling her cap over the windmill.

"What did you do?"

"I yelled 'Adelaide Sadler, go home at once!' and they jumped apart like I'd just scalded them." Godwin grinned suddenly at the recollection and his sister laughed too. But then he sobered up. "It ain't funny, Joanna," he said. "That bird-witted little care-for-nothing is bound to ruin herself. You've got to do something about it."

"I'll speak to her."

He snorted. "Famous lot of good that will do. She's never paid the slightest attention to one of your scolds, and you know it. Jack's the one you'll have to speak to. And immediately. He can send

Bert packing. And give Addie a dressing down that might do some good. He certainly seems to have the talent for that sort of thing," he added nastily. "When it comes to being disagreeable, there doesn't seem to be much to choose between him and the dear departed Gerald. Tell me, Joanna, just how did you ever manage to get mixed up with a couple of wrong 'uns like the Welbourne cousins anyhow?"

"You know perfectly well how. Our estates marched together, our fathers were fast friends, we were like one family. Besides, Jack didn't used to be so bitter. The war changed him, I suppose."

"No doubt," her brother said without much conviction. "At any rate, he's the head of the household now, not you, and he's the one to straighten Addie out. If anybody can straighten out Miss Sadler!"

"She ought to make her come-out," Joanna said thoughtfully. "Jack really should send her to London for a season. I had thought to put it off till—"

"Well, whatever." Godwin broke impatiently into her musings. "Just don't you put off telling Jack, Joanna. God knows how many of the servants already know how she's behaving. She's going to be the 'on-dit' of the neighborhood—if no worse happens to her. And tell Jack to send Bert packing," he added. "Immediately."

He left then to round up Toby, softly damning underneath his breath all bird-witted Sadlers.

Joanna sighed and climbed out of bed. She had hoped to be able to avoid Jack until dinnertime, a circumstance she was sure she could count on him to aid. But Godwin was right. This situation with Adelaide could not be ignored. The sooner she tackled Jack, the better for all concerned.

But when, after she had dressed, Joanna went in search of Jack, he was nowhere to be found. She inquired his whereabouts of Banks.

"Why, Sir John had his breakfast some time ago and went out, ma'am. That man of his would know exactly where he was gone, but he himself went into the village." Banks disapproved heartily of Dawson, the servant Jack had brought back home with him. He was a jack-of-all-trades sort of fellow, a former sergeant, who not only drove the carriage down from London but also now served as his master's valet. Banks chose to interpret his presence as an insult to the staff of Welbourne Hall. "It was my impression that Sir John was to meet the bailiff and visit some of the tenants. At least he left word that he'd want no luncheon."

Joanna was glad of the reprieve, then instantly ashamed of her relief, chalking it up as another example of her inclination to postpone all scenes. Just the same, she felt her spirits lift at the prospect of a full day of peace.

Then it suddenly occurred to her that she could use Jack's absence to good account. Gerald's old room had been prepared for him, as the biggest and the best, but he'd refused it and moved into his boyhood one instead. Whether he'd acted from nostalgia or from an aversion to anything that had once been Gerald's, Joanna did not know. She suspected that the real reason may have been the proximity of Gerald's room to hers. At any rate, the room he chose had not been turned out properly. She now decided to inspect the bed and window hangings and see if they did not need laundering.

Jack's room was in semidarkness, the curtains tightly drawn. Joanna groped her way through the gloom and whisked the window hangings wide apart, then raised the windows a few extra inches, admitting a gust of chilly air to combat the musty smell. She was halfway back across the room before she glanced toward the four-poster and turned to

38

stone. "Oh, dear God!" The words seemed frozen in her throat, a voiceless scream. Jack lay on the bed, newly awakened by the noise she'd made. He too seemed forever locked into the moment, as motionless as she. And then he jerked the counterpane over his trowser leg that lay empty from the mid-thigh down. The action came too late. It could not blot from Joanna's mind the image of a limb that ended in a stump or of an artificial leg, removed and lying there beside him.

"Oh, Coppy." The words were a sort of strangled whisper as she started toward him, arms outstretched. What she'd intended, she'd no idea. Perhaps to hold him to her breast for comfort, as one would soothe a little child. Or else to let him comfort her. But Joanna only took a step or two before she was stopped dead in her tracks by the contorted rage and hatred on his face.

"How dare you barge in here to spy on me," he hissed between clinched teeth.

"No, please, Jack—I wasn't spying." Tears welled up in her eyes. "Banks said that you'd—"

"Goddamn you, get out of here!"

"Please, Jack, don't shut me out. I didn't know. I had no idea—" Again she took a few steps toward him.

"I said get out. Damn you to hell, I don't want your pity!"

She turned her back on him then and fled. But not from fear of him. There was nothing he could do to give more pain than she already felt. But she did not want him to see her tears. No one could weep for Jack, least of all Joanna Welbourne.

She paused only long enough to snatch her cloak, then dodging down the back stairs ran outside, running till the stitch in her side slowed her to a walk. By then she had already covered much of the

39

mile that led across the park to the brook and a group of boulders beside it that she and Jack as children had called their fortress. Later on they had used it as another sort of special place.

The rock formation had been eroded before the stream had changed its course. It now formed a three-sided wall with an open view of sparkling water noisily cavorting over other, smaller rocks. Joanna crawled up into the cold stone nest and, laying her head down upon her knees, she wept. Her keening blended with the wind and noisy brook. She did not know whether it was for Jack she cried or for herself. She only knew she had not cried so since she was a child—not even when her mother died, or when Jack left, or the morning after her wedding night when she'd fled back here. Then she had vowed that she'd not return again to this special place. But now, instinctively, she'd come running back to find some balm of healing.

But it was all in vain. No sweet memories flooded over her as she sobbed into the hem of her heavy woolen cloak. Instead, when she tried to recapture what Jack and she had meant to each other long ago, she knew that those two people were now dead and gone. Whoever Jack and she, now at this moment, were, they were not the older versions of what they had been then. What might have been had died when her drunken father had taken a whip to Jack while the servants held him—and afterward when she'd turned her back on him. But still she cried.

She had no idea how long she sat there, huddled against the rock. Finally her tears were spent. Gradually she became aware that she was numb with cold, as leaden as the rock itself. She got up and climbed down to kneel by the icy water's edge and splashed her face over and over till the stinging moisture had, she hoped, reduced the swelling from her eyes. Then she turned toward home.

As much as she longed for the solace of her room, she went first to the stables and sought out Peterson, the head groom. From the way he stared, Joanna could only conclude that the cold stream had not entirely erased the ravages of her weeping. Perhaps it was just as well. He would blame her upset on this other cause, which would underscore its gravity.

"Bert is not to ride out with Miss Adelaide any more," she said.

She saw from the quick look of consternation on Peterson's face that he immediately realized why she'd issue such an order. But all he said was, "I'll see that he don't, ma'am."

"And, Peterson, will you also make it clear to Bert that unless he stays away from Miss Adelaide entirely he will be dismissed?"

"Yes, ma'am, ye needn't fear." His mouth set grimly. "He'll keep a proper distance after this."

Joanna could only hope that Peterson would keep his underling in line. For she felt that her measures had only been halfway. "Tell Jack about it and let him send Bert packing," had been her brother's remedy for Addie's indiscretion. And that was no doubt the proper course to follow, exactly what any prudent employer and guardian would have done. But Joanna could neither take that sort of action on herself or inform Jack and let him do it. She was too aware that Bert was one of a large family that depended on his wage. Starving brothers and sisters were a cruel price to pay for some stolen moments in a hedgerow.

It had never been Joanna's custom to lie down in the afternoon to rest, as many women of her station did. She usually preferred walking to erase any worries and fatigues the morning might have brought. But this day was different. The shock of discovering Jack's amputation, the fit of weeping, the scene with Peterson, and a sewing session spent with a sulky Addie carefully avoiding any topic that had to do with grooms had proven too much for her. In late afternoon she lay down upon her bed with a damp cloth over her eyes hoping that by the time she had to confront Jack at the dining table they would have lost at least some of their redness. Yesterday's dull headache had returned. What was happening to her, she wondered. She had never been prone to headaches before. They had come upon her along with Jack. She would tell him so right now, she thought hazily as she drifted into sleep. It should give him no end of satisfaction.

Right now! Joanna jerked wide-awake to find Jack standing by her bed staring down at her. At first, befogged by the unaccustomed daytime sleep, she thought he was a dream. But then she forced herself to sit upright, pushing the hair off her face and rescuing the damp cloth that had slipped down.

"What are you doing here?"

"Looking at you," he said. "At the moment a rather lowering prospect, I must observe. I need to talk to you, Joanna, and since it seems to be the new custom here at Welbourne Hall to barge into bedchambers unannounced, I followed your example. I must say though that my trespass has proven a bit tamer than yours must have done. You seem to be intact, with no spare parts lying around for me to see. No arms. No legs. How dull of you."

"Jack, stop it! Don't do this to yourself—and me. It's—macabre."

It wasn't the best possible choice of words,

Joanna realized, but under the circumstances she didn't know what would have been.

"Macabre? I beg pardon," he replied with a mocking bow. "I had not intended to be so Gothic. Or to awaken you, when it comes to that. I expected you to be dressed for dinner since the bell just rang for it."

"Oh," she said, pushing ineffectually at her hair and seeing the mess she was reflected in his sardonic eyes. "Please tell Banks to go ahead and serve. I'll only be a moment."

"I didn't stop by to escort you down to dinner, Joanna," Jack said sarcastically. "I wanted to see you in private to ask that you not mention my ... legless state to anybody else. Or have you already done so?"

"No, I haven't. But surely you don't plan to try and hide it from your family?"

"That is my intention. Though if they all possess as little respect for privacy as you do, I may be hard put to keep my secret."

"But why?" Joanna was truly bewildered by his attitude. "Why try and hide it? There's no shame in having lost a leg fighting for your country. You're a decorated hero. You should be proud."

"Proud!" His face contorted. "Proud of being a damned cripple dependent on some torturous contrivance just to walk—if you can call stumbling jerkily along the way I do walking." With some effort he got a grip upon himself and cut short what was about to explode into a tirade. "Let's just say, Joanna, that I have my own reasons for not wanting others to know about my artificial leg. Perhaps I don't wish to see the same pity and revulsion on their faces that I saw on yours this morning. Have I your word then that you'll not mention it?"

"Yes," she answered wearily.

"Very well then. I'll leave now and let you dress for dinner. And I'll tell Banks to hold the meal indefinitely, if he can. I don't wish you to have to rush. You've quite a long way to go yet if you hope to look presentable."

Chapter Five

THE LOOKING GLASS reflected Joanna's rumpled dress and tousled hair. It was easy for her to accept Jack's assessment of her appearance. Her hair, which she began to brush vigorously, was so fair that it took little imagination to color it prematurely gray. She stared harder, wondering if perhaps her face had aged and wrinkled as she slept. She might be only twenty-six, but at the moment she felt ninety. Her skin, however, was still unblemished, though ghostly pale. The eyes that stared back at her seemed enormous, ringed in dark circles as they were. She looked like a widowed owl, she told her glum reflection. Or a black-clad witch who had just run out of spells.

She flung the wardrobe open wide. There was little enough inside—a few remnants of bride clothes that seemed girlishly dated now, and of course her mourning raiment. From the former group she chose a rose-colored gown with a high waistline and small puffed sleeves. It was hardly modish and was immature for her widow status, but it had a cheerful hue. Hurriedly she put it on and brushed her hair in place, pinning it severely back then pulling a few tendrils loose to curl around her face. Before she went downstairs she surveyed the results again. Well, she seemed to be officially out of mourning now. Her rosy reflection mocked her.

Why had she ever bothered? She turned her back and walked away, not wanting to frame an answer.

They were all waiting for her, an impatient and uncomfortable assembly in the small withdrawing room. "You're late, Joanna," Toby accused, "and I'm half starved."

"Little boys are supposed to eat in the nursery anyhow," her brother observed to the chimneypiece.

"So are tutors," Toby retorted to the ceiling. "Besides, Joanna said I might eat with Uncle Jack when we're 'en famille,' so there!" This last was directed straight at Godwin's head.

Jack stood with his back to the crackling fire, sipping a glass of sherry. He looked the late arrival slowly up and down. "Congratulations, Joanna. I see I wronged you. You have managed a transformation. And in record time. I'm glad to see you out of black. I saw enough crowlike women in Spain and Portugal to last me a lifetime."

"You do look very nice, Joanna." She was rather taken aback at receiving a compliment from her brother. But then she realized that he must be grateful for the distraction her entrance had just made. For Addie was obviously in the grip of an advanced state of the sulks and kept shooting murderous glances at him from beneath her lowered lashes. Godwin tried to appear oblivious to her hostility, but his face and studied indifference betrayed him.

"From the way Banks has been peering around the doorframe, Joanna, I gather there may be a crisis in the kitchen if we do not eat immediately. You won't mind skipping the sherry?" Jack seemed to be extending himself to play the genial host. He obviously wanted no repetition of last night's unpleasantness. And also, Joanna realized, he was trying to establish himself as head of this small, oddly assorted family.

"Toby, since you are dining with the adults, act the part and take your Aunt Joanna in to dinner. Adelaide." Jack gave his niece a courtly bow and extended his arm to her. The coquette in Addie won out over martyrdom, and she gave him a dazzling smile. Sir John, his sister-in-law noted, quite forgot himself and smiled back in a manner that ill befit an uncle. It was the first time Joanna had seen him look the way she remembered him, and a lump rose in her throat. She was saved from the humiliation of misty eyes by Toby bowing and doing the polite in such a serious parody of his uncle that she giggled instead.

"You little coxcomb," Godwin muttered but he grinned as well and Joanna suddenly felt lighthearted, thinking that the dreaded evening was getting off to a remarkably good start. Then as they all proceded into the dining room, Joanna inadvertently looked to see how Jack was managing his artificial limb. He saw the direction of her glance, and the haughty stare he gave her was worse by far than any verbal set-down. The mood was shattered.

The only member of the family who even spoke at first was Addie, who kept saying, "No thank you, Charles," as the footman handed the first course around. When every dish had been waved away, much to Toby's openmouthed astonishment, she turned her martyred gaze upon the footman. "Just bring me soda water and some biscuits, please."

"Yes, miss," he murmured, his face impassive. Jack, who could not know how much Addie usually enjoyed her meals, also remained indifferent. The three others gaped at her in amazement.

"Have you gone queer in the attic?" Toby asked,

cramming his mouth with haricot of mutton. "Why ain't you eating? This is really a bang-up meal. Cook doesn't do half so well when Uncle Jack's not here. And once she's got accustomed to having him around, I expect she'll go back to her same old ways, so you really shouldn't miss it." He observed Charles's return with the menu substitution upon a silver tray. "Why you want to sit there with soda and biscuits when there's almond snow for later is more than I can say."

"I'm puzzled too," Godwin remarked innocently. Addie gave him a look that should have melted him down to ash. "If that's your idea of revenge, it's certainly an odd one. You could eat worms at dinner for all I care," and he helped himself liberally to the oyster sauce.

"What I eat, or whether or not I eat, or anything else I do, Mr. Godwin Carrothers, has absolutely nothing to do with you. I find you beneath my contempt. But since—as no true gentleman ever would—you have so rudely called attention to how I choose to dine, let me say I'm astonished that you, of all people, cannot recognize Lord Byron's regimen for keeping his weight in check. I, also, find it salubrious to fast occasionally, as do many others of the *ton* who are not of your bean-pole physique, I might add."

Godwin returned her glare for glare, for he was as self-conscious about his lack of weight as she was of her generous proportions.

"What Addie means is that she is fat," Toby translated helpfully for Jack who had settled back into his former moroseness, seeming hardly aware of the bickering going on. But at Toby's remark he strangled on his claret.

"I am not, you little monster!"

"That was most ungallant, Toby," Jack recovered

48

in time to say. "And also quite untrue. Don't you realize that your sister is well on her way to being a Diamond of the First Water?"

"What's that?"

"A beauty," Toby's uncle answered.

The little boy's eyes grew wide. "Are you really going to be one of those things, Addie?" He gazed at her with newfound respect while she turned a becoming pink.

"She's already too pretty for her own good," Godwin contributed darkly. At her look of astonishment over this oddly misfired insult, he too turned brick-red. To cover their embarrassment, Joanna changed the subject.

"Toby, what are you and Godwin studying these days?"

Any mention of lessons usually put a damper on Toby's ebullient spirits, but this time he responded enthusiastically. "Trafalger! Oh, I say, Joanna, Lord Nelson really was top of the trees! Did you know about the time he put the telescope to his blind eye so he wouldn't see the signal to withdraw? He really was a prime 'un, was he not?"

"Oh, indeed."

"In fact, I thought quite seriously for a while of enlisting in the Navy. 'Admiral Sadler' has quite a nice ring about it, don't you think? But all in all, the Cavalry really is more the thing for gentlemen."

Godwin gave a derisive snort.

"It's true!" said Toby. "Is it not, Uncle Jack? The Cavalry is rather more the thing. They do get a rather higher class of coves joining them than the Navy does. That's so, isn't it?"

"At any rate they certainly get a higher class of horses," his uncle murmured.

"Exactly. That's really what decided me against

the Navy. I'd much rather have my own horse and a Guard's uniform. A sailor can't actually look bang up to the nines the way a cavalryman can. I know it ain't so, but they really do mostly look like a bunch of slow-tops, except for admirals with that gold stuff all over them. Besides, you really do have a much better chance of becoming a hero in the Cavalry, don't you, Uncle Jack?"

"Oh, yes, indeed. The odds of heroic action are much, much greater in the Cavalry than in any other branch of the military. Why, many a man has won a resounding reputation for valor when his horse panicked and bolted into the thick of things while he was doing his level best to send the poor beast in quite the opposite direction."

Godwin choked while Addie and Joanna looked to see if Jack were serious. Toby's eyes opened with disbelief. "You're bamming me, ain't you, Uncle Jack?"

"Oh, no. 'Struth. So help me."

"Is that what happened to you then?" Toby looked as though he could hardly bear to hear the answer.

"Oh, no, certainly not," his uncle replied, cutting off another mouthful of roast duck. "As young Carrothers has pointed out, Welbournes can always be depended upon to manage their horses in expert fashion. It's only when it comes to dealing with the human race that they run into difficulty."

Since sneering mockery had crept back into Jack's voice again, the conversation died. Addie went back to feeling aggrieved, while Godwin wrestled with his guilt about betraying her dalliance with the groom. When the silence grew prolonged, Joanna reminded herself of the duties of a hostess even in a family situation and tried to introduce a new noncontroversial topic of conversation. "Godwin," she remarked brightly and falsely, "did you know that Jack was a schoolmate of Lord Byron? My brother is a great admirer of the poet," she said to Jack by way of explanation, as though they were two strangers newly introduced and she was struggling for a conversational opening.

"Indeed?" Jack hardly sounded enthusiastic, but he did turn courteously toward Godwin. "I was at Harrow with George Gordon and thought I knew him fairly well. But I must admit to some surprise when I returned to this country to find him so lionized."

Joanna knew that Jack had no intention of belittling Lord Byron by this remark. But her brother, forever on the defensive for a fellow bard, chose to take exception to what he'd said. "Why?" he bristled. "Why should it seem so wonderful that a poet might be as well known as a military hero? Writing timeless verse could perhaps be deemed just as important as killing one's fellow man."

"I merely meant," Jack replied with surprising patience, "that during our school days I was, I'm afraid, unaware of his poetic genius. But then I was not one of his intimates."

"No, I cannot imagine that you and Lord Byron had very much in common."

"That's where you're mistaken," Jack said evenly, leveling the impassioned poet with a hard black stare. "Actually we had many similar interests—" And he began to tick them off upon his fingers. "Fencing, swimming, shooting, and especially boxing. I ran into Byron more than once away from school at Gentleman Jackson's establishment. He was a great admirer of the former champion, you may know, and very handy with his fives. He liked to strip and step into the ring with Jackson and handled himself quite well. And, oh yes, we also had riding as a common interest." Joanna could not decide whether this last remark was a deliberate cut at Godwin, but by his sudden stiffening she knew that her brother thought so. "And also women," Jack continued, looking at Joanna and not Godwin. "Though of course George's successes in the petticoat line greatly eclipsed my own quite unremarkable attempts at conquest." This seemed to end his tabulation. He paused to take a sip of wine.

"You can now add one more thing that you and Byron have in common," the tutor said.

"Indeed, and what is that?"

"You both are cripples. And both take pains to conceal the fact."

Joanna had heard silence described as "thundering" or "crashing" and considered the description nonsense. It was true, she thought now. Silence could be like that. For Godwin's words seemed to split the air asunder, to hold it there, then to send the shock waves pounding back together to bombard their ears. The others sat transfixed as Jack's face slowly drained of color and his eyes began to blaze. For a moment Joanna thought that at the very least he was going to heave the contents of his wineglass in Godwin's face and at the very most attack him. And she could see that Godwin, who in spite of his slight frame and poetic tendencies was still no coward, quailed before the onslaught of emotion he'd churned up. After the silence had grown so unendurable that she thought that she must break it with a scream, Jack visibly struggled to get a grip upon himself. Calmly and deliberately he folded his napkin and stood up. "It seems to be my turn tonight to make an Edmund Kean exit from the dining table. Who knows, when I have been home a year or so, perhaps we shall contrive to finish a meal together. But now, if you'll excuse me . . ." He bowed and left. Joanna noted that he managed to hardly limp at all.

When the door closed behind Jack, the remaining four sat staring at one another, like survivors of an earthquake who find themselves miraculously still intact. "Oh, my God," Godwin groaned. "I certainly never meant to put him in such a taking. How was I to know he was so damned sensitive? His limp is very slight. Hardly even noticeable."

Joanna wanted to tell them right then just how it was with Jack, for their own sakes as well as his. But she'd given her word and so kept silent.

Then Toby heaved a heavy sigh and picked up his water goblet. He held it high, the crystal sparkling in the candlelight. "God bless England and our happy home," he said.

Chapter Six

"I THOUGHT EVERYTHING would be better once Uncle
Jack came home. Instead it's worse." Addie was sitting on Joanna's bed the morning after Jack's dinner exit while Joanna sat by the window trying to
redeem her needlework, which was looking worse
and worse.

"In what way?" she asked.

"Oh, every way. You're more unhappy than you
used to be when Uncle Gerald came home from
London." Joanna opened her mouth to deny both
states of mind, then shut it tight. Adelaide might
be young, but there was nothing wrong with her
perceptions. "And Uncle Jack and Godwin seem to
loathe each other."

"I don't think that's really true. I think they just
don't know each other yet and are dealing with
some prejudices that aren't really so. They'll be all
right in time."

"Do you think so?" Addie looked doubtful and indeed Joanna's words rang hollow even to her own
ears. "Well, I wish it could be soon, for in the meantime they keep sticking daggers in one another. I'm
afraid they'll come to blows before they ever discover each other's priceless worth." She giggled
then, but rather more from habit than from true
amusement.

"Sometimes I think I could really like him," she

continued. "Like last night when he said I was a Diamond of the First Water." She colored with pleasure at the memory. "Do you think he really meant it?"

"Oh, yes, indeed. As you've probably noticed, your Uncle Jack does not dissimulate."

"At certain times, when he's not all shut up within himself, or being starchy, it's quite easy to see why you were in love with him. He certainly is handsome, is he not?"

"Yes, he is," Joanna answered calmly, spoiling another pansy by thrusting her needle well outside the outline.

"But then all our family are quite good-looking."

"Addie!" Joanna tried to be disapproving but had to laugh at her conceit.

"Well, it's true. Even Uncle Gerald, I suppose, was good-looking in a way. Though if you cannot abide a person it's very difficult to consider him attractive. If you only saw him from a distance, say, you'd call him handsome. But up close, he was rather off-putting, don't you agree? I think he didn't look really mannish—or something. Not the way Uncle Jack does.

"But as I was saying," she backed up the conversation, "Toby's the only one who manages to feel at all comfortable around Uncle Jack. And that's only because he's so single-minded and so thick that he doesn't notice how Uncle Jack simply hates it when he goes on and on about the Army and the war. So all in all, I think things were really better before Uncle Jack came home. At least then we had great hopes that everything would be put to rights when he arrived."

"Give him time," her aunt said. "After all, he's only just got back. And he does have a great deal to contend with. Just trying to get a grasp of the es-

tate business must be a sore trial for him. This i
all much harder on him than it is on us, I'm sure

"Have you told him yet?" Addie asked abruptly

Joanna didn't pretend ignorance. She'd know
ever since Addie came so early to her room that a
other conversation was a prelude to the real con
cern, what she planned to do about the informatio
Godwin had given her.

"No, not yet."

"That odious snitch!" Addie said viciously. "I can
see why Godwin has to make everything I do hi
business. After all, since he chooses to make a per
fect cake of himself over Miss Newcomb's niece,
think he has no business getting so Friday-face
about what I do."

"Addie," Joanna said mildly, "it's hardly the sam
thing, you know. Miss Pelham's background is un
impeachable. And—well, after all—the groom!"

"Oh, I know. But still, I'll bet a monkey that th
Fair Felicia is no more interested in Godwin than
am in Bert. She's just made him one of her flirt
because there's no one else around. And he can
even see it. And as for her 'unimpeachable back
ground,' well, she may be related to an earl and a
rich as Croesus but according to Emma, who got i
from Miss Newcomb's parlormaid, she's the 'on-di
of London. They say her family has sent her dow
here on a repairing lease till some of the gossi
about her escapades dies down and they can ge
her married off. Did you know that she actuall
dressed up like a page boy and sneaked into
party the Prince of Wales was giving that she'd no
been invited to?"

"Addie, surely not!" Joanna was shocked an
hard put not to show it.

"Yes, and that was just the final straw in a whol
series of hoydenish pranks, so Emma says. So wh

Godwin has to be so proper where I'm concerned is beyond all reason. He should do his missionary work with the Fair Felicia instead of me."

Joanna sighed. "Though he has, I'll admit, some rather strange ways of showing it, Godwin really is most fond of you. I think he quite regards you as his little sister, don't you know."

Addie snorted at that, in a most unbecoming manner. "Sister! Indeed I am no such thing! Even Toby is a Pearl above Price compared to that odious—" She broke off suddenly, recalling no doubt, Joanna's relationship with the odious Godwin. "Joanna, do you really think that there's any need to tell him?"

"What on earth . . . ?" This time Addie did lose her aunt with the sudden switch of subject.

"Uncle Jack, I mean. Does he have to know about Bert and me?"

"That rather depends on you, I think," Joanna answered solemnly. "If you promise to stay away from Bert."

"Oh, Joanna, you are a trump!" She jumped up off the bed and hugged her aunt impetuously on her way out of the room. She paused with her hand on the doorknob and turned back with shining eyes. "Joanna, I've just had the most marvelous idea! You must talk Uncle Jack into letting me go to London for the Season. My Great-Aunt India would bring me out."

Lady India Claridge was Addie's father's aunt—a redoubtable old dowager and a well-established member of the *ton*.

"Why not ask your Uncle Jack yourself?"

"Because he's sure to say he can't afford it," she answered. "And Aunt India hasn't a feather to fly with any more. She can't bear the expense of my debut. So I want you to ask him."

"You overrate my influence. My asking him won't help your cause."

"Oh, but it will. You can bring pressure to bear, don't you see? If he thought it was really important, he'd dig up the brass somehow. You know he would. For it's not as if he won't get it back when I come of age."

"Yes, but I still don't see—"

"I do!" Addie's expressive eyes fairly snapped with mischief as she took a couple of steps back into the room. "Just ask him normally. And then if he kicks up a dust and says it's utterly impossible, you can play your high card."

"Whatever are you talking about?"

"Why Bert, of course! If Uncle Jack says that I can't go to London, then you must tell him that it's imperative I be sent away before I drag the fair name of Welbourne through the dust by eloping with the groom. It will work, I'm sure it will. Oh, isn't it famous, Joanna? I'll be going to London!" She laughed as she went out. "Just think of it."

Joanna did. Though Addie was not entirely bluffing and might do such a foolish thing if not given her own way, young Bert would refuse to be a party to her schemes. For Joanna did not believe him entirely wanting for good sense. But just the same, she did rather think it a good idea for Addie to make her come-out. It would be a relief if the girl contracted an eligible match before some other disaster struck. And so Joanna resolved to tackle Jack upon the subject. But not just yet. Now she needed some moments to herself, a respite from all the upsets of the last few days. She settled on her favorite method of escape. She took up her drawing pencils and her pad and went forth to sketch.

Joanna picked a hillside spot that afforded a distant view of Welbourne Hall. In the summertime she would not have been able to see the house for all the trees surrounding it. But now its solid lines were visible through a tangle of bare branches, and with an even darker slate-gray sky behind it, the prospect had a bleakness that suited her present mood. She placed a blanket in front of a low stone wall that would screen out some of the cutting wind that skipped suddenly now and then across the hills; then she sat down upon it, using the cold stones for a backrest, and went busily to work.

Although her fingers had a tendency to grow numb with cold, forcing her to pause frequently to rub them, after a busy hour she stopped to survey what she had done so far and was not entirely dissatisfied with the results. The picture was beginning to take shape in something of the form that she had hoped for, though the dream of the imagination was illusive, never to be quite realized. But the clouds swirled over the brooding hall in a manner quite compelling, so Joanna thought, though she doubted that the great Turner lay awake at nights fretting over his Hampshire competition.

She studied her creation carefully through squinting eyes, adding a touch here, removing an outline there, so absorbed with trying to translate from the mind's eye to the sketch pad that she had been hearing the thunder of hoofbeats for some time before they penetrated her consciousness. She rose to her knees to peer back over the wall and if necessary shout a warning. But the cautionary shout merged into a scream as she plastered herself back against the wall and froze in terror.

She supposed she was one of the very few persons ever to have had so good a view of the underbelly of a horse, Joanna thought wildly as the beast seemed to pause suspended there above her, legs extended in the jump, locked in time. Then finally it descended, somehow mercifully not on her. But its back hooves caught her abandoned sketchbook and sent it flying through the air. She watched in horror as the black stallion reared and whinnied in its fear, fully as panicked now as she had been.

It took some time, and no small skill, for Jack to succeed in calming him. Joanna marveled that he managed, hampered as he must have been by the artificial leg. He stuck on the rearing, lunging beast like some sort of human leech and finally soothed and coaxed it into calm. Then unfortunately, instead of riding on about his business, he wheeled back toward the wall.

"Do you realize," his voice was shaking with cold fury, "that you almost got yourself killed just now?"

"I realize that you almost killed me." Joanna was suffering a reaction of her own just then and didn't care for his tone of voice. "But I deny being any party to it."

"No party to it! Just what do you call lurking behind walls, then suddenly materializing screeching like a banshee, for God's sake? You frightened this poor animal out of his wits."

"He didn't do much for my wits either. And why I should be blamed because you chose to go sight unseen over a stone wall—"

"You know damned well that this has always been a riding course. And to crouch down out of sight is nothing short of suicidal!"

"And I should like to remind you that no one has ridden neck-or-nothing around here for years. And

I certainly cannot be blamed for not realizing—" Her voice trailed off.

"That a cripple might do so?" He fairly spit fire in his anger.

"No!" she blazed right back. Joanna hardly knew what came over her, for normally she would go to any lengths to avoid a quarrel. But the strain of the past few days plus her brush with death were taking a strange toll. For once she was not ready to shoulder all the guilt. She was fully as angry now as he. "I was not thinking like that at all. That's merely your interpretation. You choose to twist even the most innocent remark into some sly reference to the fact that you are no longer entirely perfect. Well, welcome aboard, Sir John 'Nonpareil' Welbourne. You'll have to adjust yourself to the fact that you are now just another flawed mortal like the rest of us."

She turned her back on him and went to retrieve her sketch from where it lay facedownward in the grass. Angry tears stung her eyes as she looked at the rumpled, torn page, with a horse's muddy hoofprint on it.

"At least that's no great loss." Joanna whirled to see that Jack had dismounted and was looking over her shoulder at the sketch.

"What do you mean, no great loss? It is to me. It's quite the best thing I've done."

"Really?" He squinted at it. "Well, as an illustration for one of Mrs. Radcliffe's more lurid novels, it has possibilities. But if you meant it as a representation of Welbourne Hall—well, really, don't you agree it's rather Gothic? The house you've drawn must boast two or three headless ghosts at the very least. And I hardly think the hall is haunted."

"You think not?" Joanna answered, her blaze of

fury giving way to weariness of spirit. "That just shows how much you know. It doesn't take the clanking of chains or shrieks in the night for a place to be haunted."

"Come now. You aren't about to tell me that my dear departed cousin walks at midnight? That's coming it too strong, Joanna. Gerald did not exert himself that much even in his lifetime, so I hardly expect him to come back from the grave. No, if Gerald's ghost walks," he smiled sardonically, "I'll warrant it's not at Welbourne Hall. The Queen's Head Tavern, perhaps, or some other brothel—or hovering over the faro table in a gambling hell—well, I might look for Gerald's spirit in that sort of place. For judging from the debts he piled up, that's where he spent his time."

"You just can't stop belittling him even though he's dead, can you, Jack?"

He shrugged. "His death could hardly change the fact that while he was alive we hated each other heartily. And how about you, Joanna? You never used to be an admirer of Gerald either. Don't tell me your marriage of convenience turned into a love match. I find that rather hard to swallow. Especially in light of the manner of his leaving this vale of tears. But then perhaps—"

"Perhaps I did not know that Gerald was killed in a quarrel over a Cyprian? I'm sorry to deprive you of the pleasure of telling me, but, yes, I do know of it."

"Then, if you will permit me to say so, I find this postmortem wifely devotion a bit excessive. The widow's weeds, all this talk of his wandering spirit—don't try to act a Cheltenham Tragedy for me, Joanna. We both know you married Gerald for his title and what went with it."

"That's true," Joanna answered with what dignity she could muster. "And no, the marriage did not turn into a love match. Gerald and I were both quite as miserable as you could have wished us. So rest easy on that score. And you are right. I found almost as little to like about him as you did. But you and I differ on one count. I could not despise him. In fact, I pitied him."

"Good God!" her husband's cousin exclaimed. "No wonder Gerald spent all his life in London, saddled as he was with a wife that 'pitied' him. I'd take your hatred any day."

"I've noticed that." Her anger was reawakening. "You're standing on that artificial leg right now suffering who knows how much agony rather than risk my pity or admit to any weakness. Why can't we sit down to continue this argument?"

"In the first place, you are mistaken that I'm in any sort of pain, and in the second I can see no purpose in continuing our discussion."

"I can. Not on these same lines certainly, for the past is over and done with. But I have a real need to discuss the present with you, so please come sit down and let's do it civilly." She motioned toward her blanket. "I suppose it's safe enough to sit here now. I doubt any other maniac will come hurtling over the wall."

"I was mistaken when I thought earlier that you'd not changed," he said as he sank down awkwardly upon the blanket. "You never used to be so waspish. Did marriage to Gerald do that to you?"

Joanna flushed as she too sat down, as far from Jack as the blanket would allow. "Perhaps. Among other things. But we were not going to discuss the past."

"You were not," he answered, reaching down and shifting his artificial leg a bit. "And by the by, I'll

63

admit you were right about one thing. This damned leg hurts like hell."

"Then why not remove it?"

He stared at her as if she'd suddenly sprouted a second head. "What did you say?"

"Why not take it off and ease your leg a bit. That was what you were doing when I found you on your bed, was it not?"

"Yes, but this is hardly the time or place."

"I don't see why not. There's no one here but me and we've known each other since we were both in leading strings."

He looked as though he thought her madder than old King George. "True, Joanna, we've known each other ages and at one point rather well. But I really can't recall ever removing my trowsers with you, though perhaps I've just forgotten."

"Jack, stop it!" Joanna snapped at him as she would have Toby. "Don't talk that way to me. You remember perfectly what we were to one another, so don't pretend to confuse me with any of your light-skirts. If you must remove your trowsers to take that contraption off, I'll turn my back. Just please don't be so missish."

"Missish!" the Waterloo hero snarled. "I hardly call it missish not to want to take myself apart in front of you no matter how far back we go. So let's change the subject and get on with whatever it is you need to say."

"I can't change the subject, for in part at least this very situation was what I wished to talk about. I think you should tell Addie and Toby—yes, and Godwin too—about your amputation."

"No!"

"Why not? Because they'd feel sorry for you? Why shouldn't we—they, I mean—be allowed that? After all, they care about you. And it's not as if they, or you for that matter, will go on indefinitely feeling it's the end of the world or anything. After all, you are not the first man to ever lose a limb on the battlefield."

Jack Welbourne glared at her. "By God, Joanna, if you dare to mention Lord Uxbridge to me, I promise I will unbuckle this damned wooden leg and beat you over the head with it. I heard about that heroic bastard so many times while in the surgery that I swear I wish the Frenchies had finished him off there on the spot."

Despite the grizzliness of the subject, Joanna could not help but giggle at the image he conjured up. He gave a reluctant grin.

"I can't say that I blame you," she replied. Lord Uxbridge had been a Cavalry general at Waterloo under Wellington's command. "By God, sir, I've lost my leg," he was said to have observed nonchalantly when a shell had struck him; to which Wellington reportedly replied, "By God, I think you have." And later at amputation time Uxbridge had remarked, "I have had a pretty long run. I have been a beau these forty-seven years, and it would not be fair to cut the young men out any longer." The words were on everyone's lips for months. No wonder Jack was sick of hearing of him.

"Please, Jack." Joanna took advantage of a slight softening in his mood to press her point. "You really should explain the situation to the others. They all think you've had a minor wound that will eventually heal. It isn't fair. The truth would save them awkward situations like the one last night. For, believe me, Godwin had no intention of being cruel. He had no way of knowing."

"So you want him and the others to know the truth so that they can treat me with the tact and diplomacy my invalidism calls for? No thank you,

65

Joanna. Now, was there anything else you needed to say to me? I should not be letting Ajax cool down this way." He nodded toward his horse, who was nibbling at some dried-up grass.

"Well, yes, actually." Discouraged by his dismissal of one subject, she plunged into another that she felt had only a slightly better chance of gaining his approval. "I wished to speak to you of Addie. I think you should send her to her Great-Aunt India in London and let her make her come-out."

"And is Great-Aunt India able to finance the come-out as well as be its sponsor?"

"You know she is not. You would have to charge it to the estate, to be reimbursed, of course, when Addie comes of age."

He laughed dryly. "Right now we could not charge a cockfight for Toby against the estate, let alone raise the kind of blunt it would take to launch Miss Adelaide in style. I'm sorry, Joanna," he rose clumsily to his feet, "but Addie will just have to rusticate here in Hampshire for another year or so. By then our affairs should have mended to a degree. The wait won't hurt her. After all, she is only seventeen."

"Yes, but it may not do to postpone things too long," Joanna blurted out. "You don't know Addie."

"I know what she looks like at any rate." She now had his full attention. "Is she in trouble?"

"No," Joanna said hesitantly. "Not exactly. But she might have been if Godwin hadn't seen her kissing the groom and reported it to me."

"That was certainly ungallant of our Godwin," Jack said rather nastily. "And, really, Joanna, aren't you blowing the whole thing out of proportion? I've seen Bert, of course. No doubt he was her partner in crime and not old Peterson. He's handsome enough to set a young girl's heart aflutter, I

66

suppose. But Addie is half Welbourne. I'm sure you can rely upon her knowing what befits her station. After all, it's not unusual for a seventeen-year-old to make a few unsuitable conquests. You yourself may recall a similar indiscretion. But when it comes to marrying, the female eye is always out for the best chance. Grooms and younger sons are never in it. So don't upset yourself. Addie will survive."

"Jack, you are Addie's uncle and her guardian," Joanna attempted to keep her voice calm, "so in your eagerness to give me a set-down please try not to lose sight of what is best for her. You know perfectly well there's no comparison between you and that stableboy or between our situation and theirs. So will you please quit talking fustian and bend your mind to what should be done about your niece?"

"Your point is well taken," he said. "But the fact remains that even if Addie is dallying with all the grooms in Hampshire, I still cannot afford a London Season for her. I'll have to leave it up to you to point out the error of her ways, using yourself as a model of propriety, of course." He whistled for Ajax who came trotting to his side.

"Would you like me to help you mount?" Joanna's voice was sweet, but her intent was to infuriate him.

"Why no, I'd merely like you to go to the devil," he answered just as sweetly, vaulting easily into the saddle. And it was not by accident that he turned Ajax so abruptly that Joanna had to scramble to keep the stallion from trampling her.

She stood there fuming till he was out of sight, then stooped to gather up her blanket and her ruined picture. One of Mrs. Radcliffe's illustrations, indeed! she raged as she considered what it might have been. Artistic talent is just one more thing that Sir John Welbourne has not the slightest notion of!

Chapter Seven

THE MORNING AFTER their meeting in the rain Miss Newcomb had sent around a note to Joanna inviting her, Jack, Addie, and Godwin to "family supper." Joanna had looked forward to the engagement. For one thing, any occasion that took the family from its own disastrous mealtimes could only be a welcome change. For another, she was desirous of meeting the young lady who had swept Godwin headlong into his first calf love.

They had not yet taken their seats in the Newcomb drawing room, however, before Joanna found herself forming an intense dislike of Felicia Pelham. Miss Pelham's murmured acknowledgment to their introduction was not designed to be endearing. "I have been looking forward to meeting Godwin's older sister. I understand you have been more like a mother than a sister to the poor bereaved young gentleman." Joanna could have done without the compliment since its obvious purpose was to make her feel antique. Indeed Miss Pelham glanced pointedly at the other's head as if in wonder that such a dowager failed to wear a cap to crown her years. Hearing Jack's chuckle behind her did nothing to bring Joanna into charity with Miss Newcomb's niece.

Addie fared no better. "Oh, I've longed to meet you," Miss Pelham gushed. "Godwin has spoken of a special diet that you employ. I'm all eagerness to try it for myself." Since Miss Pelham's figure was without fault, the remark must have been intended to call attention to that fact while making Addie feel self-conscious. "One cannot be too careful," she continued. "We do not wish to wind up like the Prince of Wales, do we, Miss Sadler? Have you heard the latest 'on-dit' from London? They say the Regent has taken off his corsets and his belly now reaches to his knees." She gave a tinkling laugh directed up at Jack while Addie turned beet-red at the implied comparison. They seated themselves then, the gentlemen with Miss Pelham while Addie, Miss Newcomb, and Joanna were placed an awkward distance from them. Addie shot Godwin a murderous look, in which his sister heartily concurred. Joanna felt she'd truly like to play a "mother" role and box his ears for gossipmongering.

Miss Pelham proceeded to ignore the rest of the company while she flirted with the men. Though Joanna had had no prior experience with the type, it dawned upon her that Felicia Pelham was one of those females who have very little use for their own sex. They saw every other woman as a potential rival and therefore the enemy. This bit of insight did not save Joanna from falling into Miss Pelham's trap, however. In the glare of the Londoner's sophistication she felt as dull and gauche as that lady could desire.

Miss Pelham was not, in the common way, to be termed a beauty. Certainly Addie far outshone her. But somehow she contrived to outmode the conventional standards of attractiveness. She was small-boned, delicate of feature, her hair an unremarkable light brown. But it curled in tight ringlets all around her head and was cropped quite short, to enhance her page-boy role, Joanna had no doubt. Her eyes were too protuberant to be beautiful. But their color was sky-blue and they were framed by thick dark lashes which she fluttered often and effectively, Joanna noted, in Jack's direction. She dressed in an eccentric but becoming manner, eschewing the ordinary low-cut evening bodice for a dark green velvet gown with a stand-up collar that looked almost military. Indeed she seemed to affect the tomboy in her whole appearance. Yet the result was utterly feminine, as the two moonstruck male visitors made quite clear.

But it was not Miss Pelham's claim to beauty, Joanna decided, that made her the focal point of their little gathering and, undoubtedly, of any other room that she was in. It was her vivacity of manner coupled with an air of consequence that dared one to even question whether she was the most fascinating, the most unique female ever seen. Felicia Pelham was a Nonpareil. Indeed, the term could have been invented for her.

She went on to dominate the supper conversation despite Miss Newcomb's every effort to include all her guests. Addie had withdrawn into the sulks. Her conversation was limited to requests that only "a taste" of this or that be put upon her plate. Joanna's few remarks seemed unable to rise up from a mire of the "heavy rainfall we've been having."

Her spirits had sunk in inverse ratio to Jack's obvious enjoyment of the evening. From the moment they had been ushered into Miss Newcomb's drawing room, the change in him had been remarkable. He had always been a favorite of Miss Newcomb's, and Joanna felt sure that that lady's warm greeting had done much toward making him feel at ease. But it was the London niece who deserved the greater credit for bringing him out of his black mood. For from the moment Felicia Pelham clapped eyes upon him, she set out to captivate.

Joanna found it reprehensible that an intelligent man of the world should be so susceptible to blatant flattery. Perhaps if the victim had been someone other than Jack Welbourne, she might have gained considerable amusement from observing the siren's skill. Miss Newcomb had placed Jack at the end of the table opposite herself with Felicia on his right and Addie on his left. Godwin was seated on Felicia's other side and suffered pangs of jealousy throughout the evening as she turned her back on him and her charms on Jack. Joanna could only pray she did not look quite so blue-deviled as her brother did.

The first part of the meal was spent in a lively assassination of the characters of various London acquaintances that Felicia and Jack held in common and who were, of course, quite unknown to the rest of them. Then "Oh, Major," she sighed as she leaned toward Jack, practically upon his plate, "you can't begin to know how much I envy you."

"Why?" He smiled down at her, looking infernally handsome, Joanna thought, with the candlelight reflected upon his copper hair. "Why the devil should you envy me just because I've campaigned with Freddie Rockingham?" He was the latest mutual acquaintance whose foibles they had been discussing.

"I do not mean that—as you are well aware," she replied with a deeper sigh. "I envy you your manhood. I should sell my soul to have done the things that you have done. Ah, how I long to be a man."

"What a pity that would be," the major murmured predictably. Joanna suddenly wondered just how much of Miss Newcomb's excellent wine he had consumed.

"How modest you are. You must know that all London sings your praises."

"I know nothing of the sort."

"Indeed you should. Along with Wellington and Blücher, your name is upon everybody's lips."

"Does anyone give due credit to his horse?" Godwin inquired innocently, and for the first time gained his beloved's full attention. She whirled to face him.

"How unhandsome of you to make sport of those who put their very lives upon the line so that you might be at liberty to lounge around and write your verses!"

Joanna's brother paled and appeared struck dumb.

"Godwin does not lounge around!" Addie leaped to his defense while his sister searched for a scathing set-down. "He tutors my little brother. And he has not even finished university yet. He is not old enough to—" Her voice sputtered and ran down as most likely she recalled that others younger than the tutor had fought at Waterloo.

"I think, Miss Pelham, you quite mistook Carrothers's remark about the horse," Jack said easily. "It's by way of being a family joke, from something that I said, and not intended as a slur upon those of us who fought the battle."

Joanna noted, though, that he did not look at Godwin or ask his endorsement of the Banbury Tale he told.

Its effect was instantaneous. Miss Pelham bestowed a dazzling smile upon the tutor which quite undid him. "I must pray your forgiveness, Godwin, for a most unprovoked attack. As you see, I am far too zealous in my hero worship of those who fought at Waterloo. Pray say that you forgive me."

She did not wait for Godwin's choked "of course," but turned back once more to the Heroic Major. "I know you are far too modest, Sir John, to talk of your exploits in the field, but pray tell me this at least—I've been quite dying to find out—did you perhaps attend the famous ball which the Duchess of Richmond gave?"

"I did."

"You were there? Why, Uncle Jack, you never said a word to us of having been there," Addie chimed in accusingly.

"You never asked me," was the calm reply.

"But—" Here Addie clapped her lips together and turned her attention back to the minuscule piece of partridge on her plate. What she had been going to say, Joanna realized, was that he had resented questions concerning his military life so much that none of his family dared to ask. But under the sun of Miss Pelham's adulation he blossomed forth expansively.

"Oh, pray do tell us all about it." She clapped her hands delightedly. "One hears so many conflicting stories. You are the only person that I've met who actually was there. Oh, I cannot tell you how I longed to be in Brussels! Lady Stanley had offered to take me with her party. But Papa would not hear of it. I have never forgiven him!"

Joanna could well imagine the row that had ensued upon Mr. Pelham's veto of the trip, for the fashionable world had in fact trooped to Belgium as though it were to be the scene of a carnival, not a battle. The war, all thought, had ended in 1814 when the Corsican Monster had been safely tucked away on Elba. London stayed *"en fête"* for months with the Regent hosting state visits from his allies,

Czar Alexander of Russia and King Frederick of Prussia. Then came the word that Napoleon had broken loose and was back again in France raising an army of his veterans. Wellington's Army and General Blücher's Prussians were holding Belgium while the Russians and the Austrians moved toward France's frontier on the east. Wellington was in Brussels and since it was felt it would be some time before the Corsican could make his move, the city filled up with members of the London *ton* who flocked to Belgium to be in on the excitement. Against this backdrop of mustering troops and mindless gaiety the Duchess of Richmond gave her celebrated ball.

"Well, actually, I hardly know what to say of it," Jack began. "I think for the most part the stories about the ball were quite exaggerated. There were no more than two hundred guests, for one thing, and not the 'throngs' that were reported. It's my opinion that your idol Byron," he nodded toward Godwin, "turned a rather boring affair into a legend when he wrote his famous 'On with the dance! Let joy be unconfined' account. But perhaps that's unfair. Others, no doubt, were more happily engaged than I."

"It is true, is it not, that the Duke of Wellington and most of his officers were there?" Miss Pelham interposed.

"Oh, yes. But Wellington arrived quite late. He knew by then that Napoleon was on the march, but the reports he had been given led him to underestimate the swiftness of the enemy's approach. I'm afraid that we English came close to being caught upon the ballroom floor. Fortunately a courier did arrive in time with a message for Wellington saying that Napoleon had crossed the

Sambre and had taken Charleroi. Then of course we scrambled."

"And is it true that some of the officers actually went into battle dressed in evening clothes?"

"Yes," Jack answered ruefully. "I'm afraid I was one of them. I was—uh—rather delayed, I fear, in receiving word that we were leaving."

"Ah, *cherchez la femme*, no doubt. How I envy her!" Felicia breathed, much to the disgust of the majority of her listeners. But Jack grinned rather wickedly.

"You need not. For as I told you, I found the ball to be a dull affair. In truth, after everything that transpired since, I confess to being unable to recall even what the lady looked like."

"Cruel!" Miss Pelham chided him. But then she clapped her hands delightedly. "Oh, but I can just picture you riding forth to battle in evening dress. How dashing and romantic!"

So could Joanna. As if some artist had transferred the scene onto a vivid canvas, she saw the brave young beau clad in evening clothes, hit and caught in the thick of things, his knee smalls and silken hose a crimson, pulpy mass, while his life's blood soaked into his horse's flank. She had raised her wineglass to her lips when the vision came, and her hand began to tremble and some bloodred drops spilled upon the cloth beside her plate. All eyes seemed suddenly riveted on her.

"Are you feeling quite the thing, Joanna?" Miss Newcomb asked. "You really are quite pale, child."

"I fear we've upset Lady Welbourne with all this talk of battle," Jack said dryly. He knew the direction of her thoughts and was looking like a thundercloud again.

"Indeed?" Miss Pelham gave Joanna a scornful

76

glance. "Thank heaven my own sensibilities are not quite so delicate. But let us by all means find a less disturbing topic of conversation. This time you shall choose one to your own liking, Lady Welbourne."

Miss Newcomb, however, tactfully intervened by introducing a subject of her own. And though she did so in her usual forthright manner, Joanna, who knew her well, could tell she was much out of charity with her niece. Though not nearly so out of charity as Joanna was.

"I had been intending to say that we are planning to remove to Bath next month. Dr. Hall has prescribed a course of waters for my rheumatism."

Under other circumstances Joanna might have been amused at the way Godwin's face fell and Addie's brightened at Miss Newcomb's words, but she was too concerned with trying unsuccessfully to read in Jack's face how he took the news. "I'm not sure I have the faith that Dr. Hall seems to place in the Bath cure," Miss Newcomb continued, "but I do think Bath will be much more amusing than Fairview for Felicia."

"I'm not so convinced of that as I once was," Felicia said archly with her eyes on Jack. "Suddenly the neighborhood does not appear nearly so dull as formerly." At her words Godwin looked stricken. He was, after all, part of the formerly dull scene she had resolved to quit. "But I have a famous idea!" Felicia clapped her hands. "Why do you not come to Bath yourself? You will soon be bored to distraction here and longing for other company. Please say you'll come." She placed her hand imploringly upon Jack's sleeve and gazed up into his eyes.

Those dark eyes smiled down at her. "It is something to consider," he said thoughtfully. "Lady

Welbourne has mentioned that Adelaide needs an introduction to Society. Bath might not be a bad plan for us at that."

It was quite obvious to all of them, with the possible, if doubtful, exception of Jack, that Miss Pelham had not included his family in her scheme. But there was no way in which she could civilly object. Addie, however, did not feel the same constraint.

"Bath!" she cried in the same sort of tone that an exiled Russian might groan "Siberia." "You surely can't be serious? How can you possibly think of such an odious scheme when you know quite well that I have been longing to go to London?"

"I'm sorry," her uncle said mildly, obviously preferring to postpone the discussion until they were back home again, "but I fear that London is quite out of the question for this season. I think you could learn to enjoy Bath fully as well."

"Of all the fustian I ever heard—to compare Bath to London! That really is the outside of enough! Why, nobody goes to Bath!"

While Miss Pelham obviously had no desire for Addie's company, she appeared to want Jack's sufficiently to come to his support. "Oh, I think you do Bath a disservice, Miss Sadler." She smiled a smile that never reached her eyes. "While it's quite true that Bath is not the fashionable resort it was in Beau Nash's day, I do not think you will want for amusement there. Besides, London has actually become quite flat of late."

"It might seem so to someone like yourself who has been out for several seasons," was Addie's answer. "But I should like it above all things."

"A hit, a very palpable hit," Joanna wanted to shout as Osric did to Hamlet. For though Addie, absorbed with her own grievance, had meant no insult by her reference to Miss Pelham's "several seasons," the remark obviously had struck a nerve. It had been some time since the Beauty's come-out, and Miss Pelham was in danger of being left upon the shelf. She shot Addie a look charged with venom. Then she composed herself to give a tinkling laugh. "La, Miss Sadler, you make me sound quite as ancient as the Elgin Marbles. I assure you I have not been out so long as you imply. But I have cut my eyeteeth and I do know that London can be as dull as anywhere."

"I'd like to discover that for myself. Who knows, perhaps we do not consider the same things dull —or the same people, when it comes to that."

They were almost at daggers drawn. Miss Newcomb felt the need to intervene. "Well, Bath or London, I do think, Jack, that Joanna here could profit from a change of scene. For some time now the poor child has had a great deal upon her shoulders." She smiled affectionately at her younger friend.

"I doubt, ma'am, we can persuade her to come out of black gloves just yet." Jack's voice had a slight edge to it. "Her devotion to my cousin's memory is very touching."

"But my aunt is right," Miss Pelham purred. "Though I have not her basis for comparison, it has not escaped me that Lady Welbourne looks quite drawn. It might do her no end of good to join Aunt Harriet in drinking the Bath waters." She was not going to rest the subject, obviously, and here she got a sudden ally in Joanna's brother.

"And Sir John could join the other invalids," he added nastily. "The waters might do wonders for his wounded leg." This time his wish to anger Jack could not be overlooked.

"I shall certainly have to put them to the test," Jack replied evenly, but his eyes were coldly calculating as they rested on Godwin. "Who knows. The Pump Room at Bath may outdo the Pool of Bethsaida in the Bible for its miracles of healing."

Chapter Eight

IT WAS DECIDED. They would go to Bath.

There had been an unholy row about it in the carriage returning home. Addie had put up a great fight for London. But Jack was adamant. He could not afford to frank her come-out, so she could take her choice—Bath or home.

"I choose Bath, then," she had answered sulkily, "but pray don't try to wheedle me into thinking we are going there on my account. You are only following Miss Pop-eyes."

"Miss what?" Jack inquired, choking.

"Miss Pop-eyes." Addie stuck to her guns nastily.

"Are you by chance referring to Miss Pelham?" Godwin inquired frostily. "If so, I think it shows a decided lack of sensibility to pick on the one slight flaw in an otherwise matchless—"

"Oh, you do, do you?" Addie interrupted what would have been an encomium on Miss Pelham's perfections. "And just what kind of sensibility does it take to accuse a guest in your own home of being fat? Pray tell me that!"

"She did no such thing!"

"She assuredly did. And she could not have done so if you had not been so odious as to tell her of my special diet, I might add. And she called Joanna old enough to be your mother, which was obviously done only out of jealousy and spite, for she could

81

not fail to notice that Joanna—whose eyes do not protrude at all—is easily twice the beauty she is."

"How dare you malign Miss Pelham!" Godwin's voice quivered with indignation. "She was all that was amiable to you—and to Joanna. Just because you choose to misinterpret some perfectly innocent remarks—"

"Innocent!" Adelaide laughed scornfully. "Perhaps that odious woman can pull the wool over your eyes and Uncle Jack's—and cause you both to make perfect cakes of yourselves, I might add—but Joanna and I were certainly not taken in by her. Were we, Joanna?"

"I think we should perhaps reserve our judgment. After all, we have only just now met Miss Pelham."

"Fustian!" Addie snorted. "If you did not discover in the first five minutes that she is the most cattish female you have ever met, well, you must have suddenly gone quite queer in the attic, that's all I can say. And I do wish, Joanna," she added petulantly, "that you would not always refine so upon being nice. It's really rather"— she groped for the proper word—"spiritless of you. You can't please everyone and there's no need trying to, you know."

Jack laughed rather nastily at that. "I hardly think you'll make a fighter of Joanna," he said. "After all, she's spent a lifetime trying to avoid conflict. She won't change now."

"There! You are doing it too! You are sounding like Miss Gooseberry Eyes—turning Joanna into Methuselah. She's only twenty-six, which is two years younger than yourself, I might point out."

Joanna knew that she should have been grateful for Addie's spirited companionship. Instead she was thankful for the darkness of the carriage which hid the tears that stung her eyes at both her niece's and Jack Welbourne's reading of her character. Why did she not leap to her own defense, she thought dejectedly, instead of sitting huddled miserably in the coach nursing her wounded feelings? They were right. She really was too spiritless for words.

During the next month the household settled into a shaky state of truce. All seemed determined to avoid their previous clashes and skirted around one another like wary dogs. Jack in particular perfected avoidance into an art. In the time remaining before the Bath removal, he settled in to learn all he could about running the estate. This involved long conferences with the bailiff and much riding about to see the various tenants. His evenings were spent mainly in the library—he often took his dinner alone there—where he studied the latest methods in agriculture, so Toby said, who was the only one brave enough to disturb him at such times.

Addie sulked for several days after Miss Newcomb's disastrous supper party, casting reproachful glances at her uncle upon those few occasions when she encountered him. Then, apparently deciding the Bath scheme beat being bored to death at Welbourne Hall, she began to plan a wardrobe for herself and her aunt. "Surely, Joanna, Uncle Jack won't be so nipcheese as to have us look like country dowds. He said himself that you've been too long in mourning."

Godwin somehow contrived to be absent from the dinner table those few times when Jack was there. He seemed to think he was stealing a march on his older rival by spending every possible moment with Felicia Pelham as she and Miss Newcomb prepared to leave for Bath. But since he returned from those visits more downcast than cheerful, his sister wondered if Felicia had not made it plain that it was Jack's company she desired, not his.

And, indeed, it was this preference on her part—or Godwin's fear of it at least—that almost blew the truce apart. On the evening before Miss Newcomb's planned departure, Godwin had come home in a towering rage. "Whatever is the matter?" Joanna asked him.

"I swear I'll kill that bastard yet," he replied between clinched teeth as he stormed into his room and slammed the door, leaving her standing open-mouthed in the hall.

Next day Joanna heard the explanation of his shocking conduct from another source. She was passing the open library door when Jack called out to her.

"Joanna, I'd like to speak to you a moment. Please shut the door," he said as she came inside. He motioned her to the chair she'd occupied on their previous interview. "Can't you do something about that moon-calf brother of yours?" he said abruptly. "Frankly, I'm getting a bit bored with all of his high flights. I stopped by Fairview to do the polite before Miss Newcomb and her niece left for Bath. He was there, of course as always, and showed himself completely wanting in conduct toward me. If he wants to put a bullet through me, or try to draw my cork, tell him to do so. But in the meantime, advise him to act like a gentleman instead of a sulky puppy when we are in society."

"Oh, dear," Joanna said.

"Oh, dear?" he mocked. "Is that the best you can do? I tell you I'm fed up to the eyeteeth with Godwin and if you can't convince him to mind his manners—well, I'll have to throw a rub in his way myself."

"But please, do try to understand." Though from

84

the hard set of Sir John Welbourne's jaw and the iciness of his eyes she foresaw the futility of her appeal, Joanna plunged on anyhow. "I know Godwin is behaving abominably. But look at it for a moment from his point of view. Miss Pelham is his first infatuation. He fell head over heels and began composing love sonnets from the moment he first clapped eyes upon her. And he's too inexperienced," she tried to move delicately here, not knowing Jack's own feelings, "to realize that she made him one of her flirts only because he was the sole male available and she was bored. Then when you arrived upon the scene and he saw he could not compete—well, it was a shattering blow, of course. He's been acting childishly ever since, but he'll soon get over it."

"That's absurd."

"I don't think so. He's young. Only nineteen. I can't feel that he's formed a lasting attachment."

"That was not what I meant. The absurdity is that he feels he cannot compete with me. I'm surprised that under the circumstances you have not told him of my disability. If he's thinking he's no match for me—well, that should put us on an even footing, if you'll forgive the tasteless pun."

"Fustian! What does your leg have to say to anything? I doubt you and Godwin will engage in a foot race to win Miss Pelham."

"Don't try and cut a wheedle with me, Joanna." Jack's guard was momentarily down, and she saw the misery in his eyes and felt a different sort of pain herself. He really cares for her she decided. "You know," he went on to say, "it's I who am no rival for your brother—or for anyone. For what woman wants a mutilated man?"

At first Joanna stared at him in disbelief, but then she saw that he was deadly serious. "What woman wouldn't be thankful that the man she loved came back from Waterloo alive? Even if he did happen to be crippled."

"Spare me your platitudes, Joanna. You've been married. You know what it's all about. Can you imagine anything more grotesque than climbing into bed with a man who first removes a leg and lays it aside then hops like a stork toward his waiting lover?"

"As a matter of fact, I can. Removing one's teeth or one's wig, to give but two examples which happen sooner or later to a lot of people. So I think you refine far too much upon your bit of imperfection. After all, if you are ready to tolerate Miss Pelham's protruding eyes, you should not find it too wonderful when she is not distressed by an artificial limb." Joanna stopped, aghast at what she had just said.

"Well, well." Jack appeared to be enjoying her discomfort. "Speaking of imperfection, has sweet little Joanna Carrothers suddenly developed claws? Addie will be pleased, I'm sure, to find you turned so cattish."

Joanna stood up and tried to regain some dignity as she looked straight into his mocking eyes. "I will speak to my brother about his manners. And I will not, since you insist upon it, tell him that you are an amputee." His eyes narrowed at the word but she plowed right on. "But if I were to do so, it would not reduce his jealousy one iota. Of that I'm sure. He'd still feel awkward and 'puppyish,' to use your word, around you. You are far better looking than he is—a hero—a man of the world. He has no confidence at all in being able to compete against you for the hand of a sophisticate like Miss Pelham. In fact, if you'd bother to observe it, Godwin has very little confidence in himself of any kind. You see, you've never learned what some of us have always known—that practically everyone is a cripple in one fashion or another."

"Spare me any more of your sermons," he sneered contemptuously. "You never used to be so prosy, and frankly I quite fail to see the connection between a soldier getting his leg blown off in a battle and the sort of weakness you allude to. Somehow you seem to think that because I'm crippled physically I'm supposed to understand and forgive any and all wrongs ever done me. It just won't wash, Joanna. I didn't understand greed or cowardice or betrayal when I was whole, and I understand it no better now."

"But surely those terms cannot apply to this discussion. I thought it was Godwin that we spoke of."

"Did you, indeed, Joanna?" The words were softly spoken but full of venom nonetheless.

She turned her back and left him. She tried to walk out with dignity. But Jack was, after all, a soldier. He knew when he had put the enemy to rout.

Back in her room Joanna lay down upon her bed as though suddenly taken ill. Perhaps she was ill. The viciousness of Jack's tone had hit like a physical attack. She'd known he still despised her. He'd made that point clear at their first encounter. But she had thought they'd gradually begun to work their way beyond such outbursts as they'd just been through. She knew that Jack was not one to forgive easily, but she had thought him ready to lay rest the past. Now she saw that his humiliation had cut too deeply for him ever to recover. Gerald was scoring over him once again.

They had always been in conflict, she recalled. The cousins had despised each other heartily. Gerald had lorded it over the younger boy on two counts—family and inheritance. His mother had been the daughter of an earl, Jack's an Irish governess. And Gerald could never let Jack forget for a single moment that it was he who was destined to be Sir Gerald Welbourne, Lord of the Manor, as it were.

But the older cousin was not content to keep his bullying on the verbal plane. Joanna had dreaded Gerald's school holidays for weeks in advance, knowing the hell he would create for the younger boy. And during them Jack had borne the welts and bruises of many a brutal encounter that no one but herself had ever seemed to notice. She pleaded with him to let Gerald have his way, but he refused to knuckle under to the bigger boy. Indeed she never doubted for an instant that Coppy would let Gerald kill him before he'd cry "enough."

Later on the tables had turned dramatically. For it was Jack who became the athlete and the fighter. Gerald had had to resort to subtler means to gain ascendancy. Joanna had been the final pawn in their game of Cain and Abel.

Somehow Gerald had learned of their planned elopement. Joanna suspected that her maid had told his valet, though afterward the maid swore that she had not. However he had learned of it, Gerald carried the news to Joanna's father, then offered for her hand.

At first she tried to stand up to the both of them. Even if he stopped the elopement, she told her father, she would not agree to this other marriage. He had been drinking heavily, as usual, and was in a towering rage. He had picked her up bodily and locked her in her room. Then he left with Gerald and two back-up servants for the posting house, where Jack had gone to hire the rig that was to take them to Gretna Green.

They had come wheeling noisily into the busy inn yard, Joanna had learned later, and Gerald had shouted for all the locals as well as the travelers to hear, "You're wasting your blunt hiring that shabby rig, Irishman. The lady's had a better offer."

Jack leaped straight for his cousin's throat. It had taken both servants plus Joanna's father to pull him off. Then after they had tied Jack to a hitching post, Joanna's father had horsewhipped him in front of the gaping crowd for "dragging my daughter's name into the mud."

But Jack had come for her anyway. Later on that night he had sprung his horses up the circle drive of Blackthorne and pounded upon the door. He had pushed aside the footman who tried to stop him and had stood in the hallway in the lamplight, pale as death with the marks of her father's whip streaked across his face. He had shouted for Joanna to come down, while the servants gaped in terror and her father had gone running for his gun. She had appeared at the head of the stairs in her nightdress and told him that she could not go with him.

She had wanted to explain it all. To tell how her mother had unlocked the door when her father left and had wept and wrung her hands and talked of Joanna's duty and of her own poor health. "People of our class cannot allow themselves to be swayed by love," she'd said. Godwin's future rested upon the help that Gerald offered for their encumbered estates. Besides, how could she be so heartless as to desert her mother now—abandon her to cope alone with her drunken husband? Joanna had wanted to tell Jack that though she loved him and always would she had no choice in what she did. But she never got the chance. "I'm not coming," was all she ever got to say.

"Then marry him and be damned to you," he had answered and turned upon his heel, walking past

89

her father and his pointed gun without ever seeing them.

Later there had been the bitter, accusing letter which she had burned but not managed to forget. Over and over in her mind she had refuted all his terrible accusations. Most of them had come by way of Gerald, making him believe she'd leaped at the chance when marriage to the title had been offered her.

Joanna had tried to explain her reasons in a letter that months afterward was returned to her unopened. But in spite of all denials, her conscience whispered, "Could he be right about me—at least in part? Could all my high-flown excuses of sacrifice and duty simply boil down to this—that when the time of crisis came, I had merely, as was my habit, chosen the path of least resistance?" Had she had the spirit and the daring of a Felicia Pelham, she thought now bitterly, she would have gladly thrown her cap over the windmill and run to the ends of the earth with him.

And indeed, time after time she had dreamed she reached that point again when he shouted for her to come and she stood poised at the head of the staircase looking down into the pale, marked face and the burning eyes. He held out his arms to her and she went racing down. Always she awoke in tears to remember it did not happen so.

Chapter Nine

Against all odds, Joanna would have said, a remarkably cheerful party drove into Bath in early spring. Jack had chosen to bring his own curricle rather than risk what the Bath stables might have for hire and so went on ahead. Addie, Godwin, Toby, and Joanna, spared his dampening presence, had been like school children let out on holiday, as indeed one of them truly was.

It was largely Toby's enthusiasm that made them so lighthearted. The entire party partook greedily of the gingerbread and apples he had brought along. And they listened with interest to his preview of the "bang-up" things he planned to do in Bath. In fact, they had great difficulty persuading Toby of the necessity for going straight to their rooms and settling in before visiting Pulteney Bridge or Sydney Gardens.

It was the choice of those rooms, Joanna thought, that turned Addie around from denouncing Bath, "a place fit only for invalids and retirees," to deciding that she might tolerate a visit there after all, "though of course it could never compare to London." Shortly after he'd made up his mind to go there, Jack had sent Banks to hire a house. The butler had succeeded in obtaining apartments in the Royal Crescent.

"But can we afford to stay there?" Addie had blurted out anxiously.

"No, not really. But if we're all to go on the Marriage Mart, it won't do to be clutch-fisted. Appearances are everything, you know. I've concluded that the only way out of Dun Territory is for all of us to dangle after wealthy spouses—with the exception of you, of course, Adelaide. In your case all our energies must be spent in keeping other gazetted fortune hunters away. Which puts us in an equivocal position, to say the least.

"But at any rate, I felt the Royal Crescent would be an ideal spot for Godwin, Joanna, and myself to flush out suitable nabobs, or their sisters or daughters as the case may be. Unless, of course, the Crescent is filled with other down-at-the-heels adventurers like ourselves."

"Uncle Jack, you are perfectly outrageous," Addie had chuckled as she jumped up from her chair to throw her arms around him in a bear hug that obviously both surprised and pleased him. "I don't care what flummery you talk. I shall like being in the Royal Crescent above all things."

If Joanna privately thought that Jack had chosen their situation more to please himself than Addie, she certainly was not about to say so. But as they swung into Bath and veered right off the London Road just before it would have led them on to York House, and then drove past the Assembly Rooms, through the Circus and a short distance further to the Royal Crescent, she could see that their location would provide easy access to many of Bath's favorite meeting places, even for a man with an artificial leg.

"It's just as well that we're not to go to London," Godwin jeered as Addie, Toby, and Joanna "oohed" and "aahed" their way into town. "A real metropolis might have undone you altogether."

It was hard for Joanna to imagine that the capital could have eclipsed Bath in any way but size. The town with its Abbey Tower and church spires and granite pavements and lovely residential squares truly was magnificent. Everywhere she looked, the architects had made use of the local oolite stone, of a pale golden color that fairly sparkled in the sunlight. But when the coach turned onto a broad cobbled carriageway and came to a halt in front of a row of gently curving town houses, the Crescent's white glare seemed to outshine any of the wonders they had seen before.

"We're here!" Toby whooped and fairly fell out of the coach to rush toward an open door where a smiling Banks and an impassive Jack were waiting to welcome them. The rest of the party, however, paused to goggle openmouthed at the younger John Wood's architectural masterpiece that was to be their temporary home. There were thirty of the adjoined houses, Joanna found out later, but the continuous cornice, plus the parade of great Ionic columns which supported it, gave the semblance of one long lovely structure curving into a graceful semielipse. The concept was simplicity itself, yet magnificent. The Royal Crescent richly deserved its name.

"Oh, Uncle Jack, it is handsome of you to have brought us here! This really is bang up to the nines!" Addie flung herself upon her uncle, sending him reeling in the process. "We'll be as up to snuff as anyone in Bath! Just imagine—giving our direction to the Royal Crescent!"

"Well, if you are so wanting in conduct as to talk continuous cant," Jack grinned down at Addie, "no bang up to the nines Corinthian is going to inquire as to your direction."

"Don't put yourself into a taking over my conduct," his niece giggled back at him. "I intend to be as proper and ladylike as—as—Joanna!"

"Oh, come now. You needn't get quite as starched as that," Jack answered dryly while Joanna felt her cheeks begin to burn.

Then she saw that he regretted the hateful words. For Jack too seemed to feel the need to turn over a new leaf where the family was concerned. At least Joanna wondered if that was not part of his reason for removing them to Bath, to get them all off to a fresh start after the muddle they had made of it at Welbourne Hall. At any rate he reverted quickly to his former bantering tone.

"I'm glad you feel that it's handsome of me to have brought us here, for I've already commandeered the best bedchamber for myself. The rest of you will have to make do with whatever's left. Banks here will show you all around."

Toby, though, had not waited for any invitation to explore. He had rushed past them in the hall and up the staircase, where the sound of his running boots echoed from the upper levels. Then he had charged back down to explore the ground floor last. Now he materialized by Joanna's side and gave her hand a tug. "There's a chimney sweep in there," he said, gesturing back along the corridor from whence he'd come.

"My apologies, ma'am," Banks said, looking most annoyed. "When I lit the fire in the library this morning to rid the place of damp, a blaze started in the chimney. I felt it necessary to send out for a sweep." His tone spoke volumes about the poor housekeeping practices that had allowed such a situation to develop.

"Come with me, Joanna. I want to see." Toby looked up, round-eyed and pleading.

"Run on then," Jack said to him. "They won't object to being watched. I'm sure your aunt would like to forgo the treat and settle in first." He was trying to gloss over his previous lapse of manners by taking Joanna's part, but Toby was persistent. "Please." He gave Joanna another anxious tug.

And then she understood. Though wild horses could not have dragged the admission from him, Toby was afraid. A terrible tale had recently come to light of an upper class little boy who'd been stolen by a gypsy, then sold for a chimney sweep. The story was especially terrible in that it was not unusual. Before Joanna realized what was happening and put a stop to it, Emma had used the threat of gypsies and the terrible fate of little climbing boys to control Toby's behavior. "Bad little boys get took by gypsies," was what Joanna actually heard her say. Now Toby pulled at his aunt's hand, victim of a morbid fascination.

"Oh, very well," Joanna said while Jack shrugged at her acquiescence. She allowed herself to be pulled into the library just as a pair of sticklike sooty little legs appeared, to dangle a moment in the Rumford fireplace, then drop down upon the hearth. A begrimed and pathetic urchin, looking indeed more like a monkey than a child, crouched on the hearth and stared up at them through frightened eyes that stood out like two white saucers in the blackened face. Soot rained down around him while his only slightly less grimy master stuck his head and shoulders up the chimney to inspect his charge's job.

Toby, who had been giving the urchin—a boy much smaller than himself but probably his age—stare for stare, seized the opportunity of the older sweep's partial disappearance to hiss, "Quick, tell me who you are."

The child, made even more terrified by the small "swell's" conspiratorial tone, could only drop his jaw a bit.

"Hurry and tell me." Toby's hiss grew louder still. "Tell me who you are. Perhaps I can help you."

" 'Erbert," the tiny lad gasped, disposing of his origins, to Joanna's mind at least, by those two syllables. But not for Toby.

"Where do you come from?" he persisted.

"Lunnon," was the answer.

"Before that, I mean. Who are you really?"

But the boy's master had extracted himself from the chimney to scowl at the nobs.

"Wot do you mean, 'oo is he really?" he asked belligerently. " 'E's me third boy, that's 'oo 'e is and the most worthless climber o' the lot." He glared at 'Erbert while the poor child looked more frightened than before, a feat Joanna would have thought impossible. "I can tell ye this—I never once 'ad to light a fire under his brothers to send 'em up a chimly, but this un's so hen-hearted as to pass belief, and there's the truth of it," he finished up contemptuously.

"Well, how would you like if it someone set a fire under your feet?" Toby retorted stoutly while Joanna nervously wondered as to the whereabouts of Jack or Banks. "You wouldn't like it above half, I'll bet a monkey. And besides"— suddenly he'd found his own courage in the process of championing a cause—"I don't believe 'Erbert's your boy at all!"

"Toby!" Joanna was horrified.

The chimney sweep glared at them. "Oh, he's mine, right enough, the more's the pity. And 'e wasn't stole and 'e wasn't bought, I'll tell ye that much if that's what ye're a thinking."

A throat cleared and Joanna turned thankfully to see Banks standing in the doorway, giving the sweep an icy stare. "If you're finished now . . ." he prodded haughtily.

The sweep began to gather up the various brooms and brushes of his trade, mumbling all the while about how it was hard enough to make an honest living without having every bleeding-heart reforming gentry-cove accusing him of stealing his own flesh and blood. Joanna gave Toby's hand, which had never left her own, a prompting squeeze and retreated with him toward the hall. But in the doorway Toby stopped and turned around. "Good-bye, 'Erbert," he said solemnly.

Surprisingly a smile broke through the urchin's blackened face. "Good-bye yerself," he mumbled.

"Let's go choose our rooms now," Joanna said to Toby. But just as she was set to mount the stairs and see what Addie and Godwin might have overlooked, the doorbell sounded. Banks paused to give her the opportunity to follow on Toby's heels and disappear upstairs. "Go on and answer it, Banks," Joanna said resignedly. He opened the door to admit Miss Pelham, accompanied by a most wonderful apparition.

She'd only just arrived in Bath, Joanna thought, and already she was face-to-face with a Corinthian or a Buck or a Bang-up Balde or a Dandy or a Beau—words failed her as she watched the gentleman hand Banks his conical beaver, more like a gigantic toadstool, she thought, than like a hat, and then remove his yellow greatcoat, hung with capes too numerous to count.

"Ah, Lady Welbourne, I can see that you are just going out." Miss Pelham eyed Joanna's old pelisse, suddenly made shabbier by her own stylish walking dress. Then she added with real sincerity, "Pray do not let us interrupt your plans. We only stopped a moment hoping to find Jack at home. And to welcome all of you to Bath, of course," she tacked on as an afterthought.

Jack indeed, Joanna thought. What had happened to Major Welbourne or for that matter, to Sir John? "You quite mistake the matter. I was not leaving," she answered sweetly, glad to see the other's disappointment. "We have only just arrived. But allow me to offer tea."

"May I suggest the gold drawing room at the head of the staircase on your left," Banks murmured.

"Lady Welbourne," Miss Pelham recalled her manners, "allow me to present Captain Maximus Rees, a particular friend of mine, just down from London."

"Lady Welbourne," the captain murmured and bowed low over Joanna's hand, allowing her the opportunity to observe him closely, though gawk was more precisely what she did.

For here was a male totally outside the range of her experience. Jack dressed very well, or so Joanna had always thought, with coats by Weston and boots by Hoby, but his was a quiet elegance. Gerald had been a bit more careless in his dress than Jack, and more inclined to try out the latest starts of fashion, but at his most daring he was no match for this exquisite now before her.

Captain Rees's coat of superfine, a most amazing lilac color, was so padded at the shoulders and so nipped in at the waist as to defy anything that nature had had in mind at his creation. His neckcloth was twined all the way up to his ears but even so was topped by shirt points so stiffly starched that they might have caused his cheeks an injury had it been possible for him to turn his head. His hair—a dullish brown, a sore trial, Joanna guessed, for such a peacock—was swept artfully into little points around his face in a geometric echo of his collar. A sprigged waistcoat, yellow pantaloons, gleaming boots adorned with golden tassles and blackened with champagne in the manner of Beau Brummell, completed his ensemble. Then to gild the lily, he was hung with chains and fobs and rings and quizzing glass.

Joanna was so taken with this Pink of the *ton*'s adornment that his face came as a complete surprise when she finally got around to looking at it. A pair of knowing pale blue eyes twinkled at her as they read her mind. The rather small mouth in his nearly handsome face pursed in mock disapproval, like a governess forced to prod a favorite child to recollect her manners.

"How do you do?" Joanna said.

"Enchanted," he breathed back.

Addie, Godwin, Jack, and tea arrived simultaneously in the gold drawing room. Joanna was both touched and exasperated to see how her brother's eyes lit up at the sight of Felicia Pelham. That lady chose to single him out immediately and draw him down beside her on the small settee while she murmured inquiries about his muse and hoped rather loudly that she still figured somewhere in his inspiration. It was cattish, Joanna admitted honestly to herself as she poured out the tea, to suspect that Miss Pelham's sudden absorption with the poet was entirely for Jack Welbourne's sake. Her suspicions were confirmed, however, when Felicia jumped up and left Godwin, mid-stanza as it were, to carry a cup of tea to Jack who was standing by the mantel. "We've come to fetch you," she said archly to him.

"Maximus needs advice about some cattle he's determined to acquire. I say that he's sure to be fleeced by some Jack Sharp, but still he refuses to take advice from a mere female, even though he's known by all to be a perfect clod-pole when it comes to judging horseflesh."

"Oh, I say now, that's cutting it rather rough," Captain Rees protested amiably. He had risen to offer tea to Addie, who had been the sole object of his rapt attention since introductions had been made. His admiration for her was written large. Addie, on the other hand, looked unable to decide whether to be amused or overawed by all his elegance. Since her knowledge of both the world of men and the world of the *ton* was rather limited, awe seemed to be winning out.

"Not a bit of it," Miss Pelham countered. "You should see the broken-winded jade pulling his gig right now. I vow I'm mortified to be seen riding with him. Major Welbourne, if you had not unhandsomely ignored my suggestion that you find a situation in our neighborhood, I should never have consented to set foot in Maximus's rig. Why did you choose the Royal Crescent, by the by?" She cast a rather disdainful glance about the apartment which Joanna had up till then considered elegant. "The new Bathwick Estate is really much more fashionable."

Jack shrugged off the question by saying he'd left all that sort of thing to Banks; then he tactfully switched the subject back to horses.

Joanna found herself feeling more in charity with him than she had for quite some time. They might have been living in Laura Place cheek to jowl with Miss Felicia Pelham. She shuddered with a pang of guilt for not wishing to be near her oldest friend. But even the considerable affection she felt for

100

Miss Newcomb could not override her great aversion to her niece. This new encounter seemed destined to increase rather than reduce the dislike she felt.

"So you must save me further humiliation by driving me to Montpelier Row in your curricle." Felicia smiled up at Jack. "Maximus may trail along behind and observe what a bang-up rig looks like. Then when the usual assortment of nags that all horse dealers reserve for him are offered up, he'll have a basis for comparison. I think even Maximus cannot fail to observe the difference in your matched grays and the specimens they'll try to foist off on him. Please say you'll come and throw a rub in the way of all those sharpers just lying in wait for poor Maximus."

Jack laughed and rang for a servant to bring his rig around while Captain Rees turned his imploring gaze on Addie. "Now then, Miss Sadler," he said in mock seriousness, "you've heard that heartless female's slander. Pray take pity on me and say that you aren't too proud to accompany me in my most respectable, I assure you, if not quite modish gig. I understand that you yourself, like all the Welbournes, are no mean judge of horseflesh. And I'm sure I can rely upon you for sympathetic understanding. Indeed if we do follow along behind as Felicia suggests, we may contrive to find that your Nonesuch uncle is in fact cow-handed."

Addie was all eagerness. But she turned a doubtful look toward Joanna which Felicia Pelham was quick to deal with. "I'm sure that Lady Welbourne must be fatigued. And I know that Godwin's demanding muse quite longs to see the last of us."

Neither Godwin nor Joanna managed a reply, but none of the others noticed this omission as they scrambled into coats and cloaks amidst much good-natured bickering about the various points to keep in mind while choosing horseflesh.

When the last footstep had sounded down the stairs and the echo of the closing door had reached them, the brother and sister still sat balancing their empty teacups. "Who'd have thought we'd ever be residents of Bath," Godwin finally remarked hollowly.

"Yes, it's ever so exciting, is it not?" Joanna's tone quite failed to match her words. "More tea?"

Chapter Ten

TOBY AND JOANNA set out next morning to buy Bath buns. It had seemed futile for her to mention lessons to him. Besides, Addie had bespoken Godwin to accompany her "directly to the Pump Room as soon as it should open." So, though Joanna was by no means settled in, she had little wish to dampen the enthusiasm of a child now fairly dancing with delight. She could only hope that some of Toby's high spirits would be contagious. Her own mood was decidedly blue-deviled. Ever since Jack and Addie had returned from the horse-buying expedition, Addie in stitches over the drolleries of Captain Rees on the subject of the bullying Miss Pelham and her grinning uncle looking like the young man Joanna used to know, she had been in the dumps. Why Jack's recovery did not please her more she could not say.

But at least Toby worked as a tonic. In spite of a cloudy day and the puddles and mud from a previous rain that they splashed through or dodged, as they threaded their way through the maze of carriages, chairs, and pedestrians that thronged the route to Milsom Street, Toby's excitement mounted. Once they'd reached Molland's Pastry Shop and had consumed a bun apiece and then had bought two more for Toby to eat en route back home, Joanna's spirits had also begun to rise. She had not yet drunk the famous medicinal Bath waters and so was no true judge of them, but she wondered if Bath buns might not be the more beneficial—at least to wounded spirits.

Aunt and nephew slowly made their way back toward the Crescent with Joanna resisting Toby's schemes to visit Sydney Gardens that very minute. "We can't do everything the first day, Toby." At that point they were walking through the Circus, a complete circle of houses designed by John Wood the elder and finished by his son. Joanna was gawking at the three tiers of columns on the buildings, which were, so she had been informed by Banks, of the three classical orders—Doric, Ionic, and Corinthian. She was trying to sort out which was which when Toby, trailing along behind her, roared "Joanna!"

She turned to see an enormous dog of uncertain origin sitting on its haunches licking its lips and staring up at Toby expectantly. If a dog could be said to smile, this one did. Certainly his tail brushed the dirty cobblestones joyfully. "He ate my bun!" wailed Toby. "It was my very last one."

"Wellington! How could you! You worthless cur, will you never learn your manners!" a deep voice called behind them. They turned to see a tall man in a dark greatcoat, which Captain Rees would have found sadly lacking in capes since it boasted only two, hurrying toward them. He snatched a curly beaver off his head, exposing fair hair cropped fairly short in no particular style that Joanna recognized. She noticed particularly the smiling gray eyes in a pleasant though not precisely handsome face. "Please accept my apologies for Wellington's total want of conduct," he said to Toby, who was staring aggrievedly at the hopeful dog. "The blame actually is mine. I should have had

104

him on a lead. You see, I keep operating under the illusion that I have him trained to stay docilely at my heels. And of course nothing could be less true. Particularly in the event of his spying a Bath bun. He has an almost sinful weakness for them. But now Wellington," the tall man spoke sternly to the dog, who reluctantly shifted his eyes from Toby to his master's face. "You thief, at least beg the young gentleman's pardon."

At this, the animal obediently sat back upon its haunches and raised its paws upward in supplication. And in spite of being so aggrieved, Toby laughed delightedly. "Why do you call him Wellington?" he asked the smiling gentleman. "I mean to say, do you think it suits him?"

"Not at all, I'm afraid," Wellington's master said ruefully, seeming to squint at his scruffy mongrel through a stranger's eyes. "But you see, I found him as a puppy on the Peninsula after a skirmish we'd had there. His mother had abandoned him in the fighting, I suppose. At any rate, he was miserable and scared and half starved and such a pathetic-looking little mite that I felt he should have something heroic to aim for. So I called him after our commander. But I'm afraid that his resemblance to the Iron Duke is nil—except perhaps when it comes to size. You must admit his proportions are heroic."

"I think he's a brick," Toby pronounced solemnly. "I've never known a military dog before. And I really think he's quite distinguished looking in his way."

Wellington jumped up just then and licked Toby joyously on the face, sensing perhaps that he was no longer in the boy's black books or perhaps merely noting the remnants of Bath buns upon his lips. Whatever the motive, the friendship was well sealed. Toby threw his arms ecstatically around the dog, fairly "nice-boying" the poor animal to death.

"Wellington is saying that he intends to replace your bun, of course. You will turn back to Molland's with us, will you not, and let us make amends?" The stranger smiled down at Joanna in a most charming fashion.

Before she could form her regrets, Toby intervened. "I say, my uncle was on the Peninsula too. Do you suppose he knows Wellington, Joanna?"

"Well," she answered, "he knows the Duke, of course. But I'm not so sure of this one. Perhaps. He certainly is equally as memorable."

"What regiment is your uncle in?" the stranger asked.

"Oh, he's not in the Army any more. He was wounded at Waterloo. He's a hero, don't you know, but he won't tell me about it at all which is really rather shabby. But he was in the Cavalry. The Household Brigade. Did you perhaps know a Major Welbourne?"

"Jack Welbourne!" The stranger looked incredulous. "Good lord, you're Jack's family! Know him! Why we campaigned for six years together. There's no one I'm prouder to call friend. Lord, I can't believe it! Is Jack in Bath?" After exclaiming a bit more about the smallness of the world, Wellington's master rallied to introduce himself. "I'm Major Charleton Russell, ma'am, and are you Jack's sister then?"

Joanna explained that she was Jack's cousin's widow and then listened uncomfortably to the major's embarrassed condolences. After that nothing would do but that they should walk back to Milsom Street and let the major atone for Wellington's thievery. Joanna protested their need to return for Toby's lessons but was shortly overridden. Toby looked so horrified at the prospect of being parted from Wellington that she had not the heart to be so cruel. Besides, she was not that eager to return herself. For she could not fail to realize that the major's interest in the excursion was not entirely inspired by Bath buns and little boys. And after the rebuffs her esteem had taken in the past few weeks, she found the attentions of the attractive military gentleman more than a little flattering.

And so they turned again to Milsom Street, this time with Toby in charge of Wellington and the major and Joanna bringing up the rear. The conversation dealt almost exclusively with Jack. All that former soldier's reticence and modesty were made worthless in the space of half an hour as Major Russell spun one anecdote after another to illustrate Major Welbourne's bravery while Toby fairly glowed with pride. Joanna lived in fear that the battle descriptions would grow too graphic for Toby's ears. The major noticed her anxiety and looked concerned. "How is Jack getting along now, with his leg, I mean," he asked.

"Oh, it scarcely seems to bother him any more," she answered brightly and no doubt falsely for the major gave her a puzzled look. She managed to shake her head warningly at him when Toby wasn't looking.

He changed the subject then and explained that he was now on leave. It seems that he was one of Nature's rarities—a Bath native and not a visitor—and that he was staying with his mother in Landsdown Crescent and would be in Bath for several weeks, he hoped, since there was little enough for a cavalryman to do now that Boney was safely scotched.

Later when Joanna got the opportunity as Toby and Wellington shared a new supply of buns, she whispered, "I hope you will say nothing about Jack's leg, Major Russell. He does not wish his amputation known. I only found out by accident myself. The rest of the family thinks he was only slightly injured."

He stared at her. "My God," he breathed. "But why?"

She was spared trying to answer the unanswerable and merely shrugged as Toby spoke through a mouthful of bun, "Oh, I say, Joanna, I know that Wellington would like the labyrinth above all things. It's bound to be a bang-up sort of place for a dog to visit."

"No," she said repressively. "We absolutely must go home right now."

"Tomorrow then?" The major grinned. "Wellington has been teasing me unmercifully to go. I have a capital idea. Why do I not call for you at ten? We can attend the public breakfast, then lose ourselves in the maze to our hearts' content."

Joanna hesitated, wondering about the propriety of such a scheme.

"Oh, please say yes, Joanna," Toby begged. "I should like it above all things. And you did say we'd go soon. And it would be invaluable to have Wellington along—for an experienced campaign dog is certain to be able to find his way out with no difficulty at all. His instincts are sure to be true."

"Undoubtedly," the major rejoined solemnly. "But I tell you what. Why don't you allow Lady Welbourne to consult your uncle first? Then if he vouches for me, as I'm sure he will, I shall pick you up at ten. If he disapproves of me as an escort, then he can meet me at the door and throw me out himself."

After that, Joanna could raise no possible objection, nor did she desire to do so. They parted on those terms, the major having reluctantly admitted that he was engaged to meet his mother in the Pump Room, quite some thirty minutes before, to be accurate.

No sooner had they arrived back home than Toby went clattering through the house to find his uncle. "Here he is, Joanna," he whooped from the library as she trailed in behind him. Jack sat in a wing chair reading the *Bath Chronicle* with his legs outstretched upon a footstool. His face had that look of strain that she'd come to connect with pain, but it relaxed into a smile when Toby announced that they'd just met a particular friend of his, a Major Russell.

"Old Charlie here? My God, I'd quite forgotten. He actually comes from Bath! Born and reared here, he said. Didn't know anybody ever was."

"And did you know Wellington?"

"My lord! Don't tell me that he still has that mongrel with him!"

Toby took immediate exception to such a shabby description of the canine veteran. "Wellington is not a mongrel. How many other dogs do you know that have seen Army service? Not one, I'll bet a monkey."

Jack gravely begged his pardon for seeming to malign such a noble beast. "Truly, I'm all admiration for Wellington. I've shared my mess with him on more than one occasion."

"Have you, by Jove? So have I." And Toby told him about the buns while his uncle chuckled.

"I say, Joanna," Jack suddenly looked quite thoughtful, "I think I'll introduce Charlie to Adelaide. I believe he'd like her. She really is a taking little thing, at least when she comes down off her high flights. And I'm none too pleased with the way

Rees has started dangling after her. Do you know he's been here twice this morning looking for her?"

"Twice?" Joanna echoed since an answer seemed expected and she'd nothing else to say.

"Yes. I've my suspicions that Felicia is throwing him at Addie's head. She vouches for him, of course, but I have some reservations. I've the feeling that underneath all that buffoonery he's actually too knowing by half. For instance, a less clever fellow might have tried to pull the wool over my eyes about his military background. But he must have known he couldn't hope to cut that kind of wheedle. So when I asked him what regiment he'd been in, he answered cool as could be, 'Good lord, none of course. You military chaps are always being shot at. Not my sort of thing at all, old man.' He said he'd just taken the title captain because it sounded more dashing than plain Mr. Rees," Jack chuckled. "Really it's hard not to like the fellow, but I don't want Addie entangled with him. Now Charlie would be the very thing for her. He's a steady chap. About a year older than I am, I believe. And he looks well enough, I suppose. I don't know how women judge such things. Would you call him handsome?"

"Near enough as to make small difference," Joanna answered. If her tone was a bit reserved, he took no notice.

"Well, that settles it then. We'll throw the two of them together and see what comes of it."

"Addie could come with Joanna and me to Sydney Gardens tomorrow," Toby chimed in helpfully. "We're going to the public breakfast and then the labyrinth—or at least Major Russell said we might go if you'd vouch for him and I know you will. So Addie could come too. Though I really don't think Major Russell will like her above half. She's much too shatter-brained. And she's not actually a Diamond of the First Water yet, you said. Besides, I think he already likes Joanna. I think he likes me well enough and he might have taken me to the labyrinth, but I'll bet a monkey that the breakfast idea was on account of Joanna instead of me," he finished up ingenuously.

The atmosphere had cooled considerably during Toby's speech. Jack stood up and laid his paper down. "Fast work, Joanna. You certainly have wasted little time in getting your hooks into a new victim. I should tell you though—Charlie's no catch for you. He has a competency, no more. Don't rush your fences. You've just arrived. There's still the Pump Room and the Assembly Rooms to be explored. Better yet, why don't you check the hospital for some rich ancient invalid? Then you'd not have to put up with him any longer than you did Gerald."

Joanna stood mute while he flayed her with his words. Why couldn't she lash back like other people did when they were attacked? she asked herself. Why did the first skirmish always have to be waged against herself to keep down the tears and not add disgrace to pain? She was far too easily a victim. She never even managed to bring her forces into action.

Toby, however, suffered no such handicap. He stood staring at his uncle, astonished at his unaccountable switch in moods. He then took one quick look at Joanna and rose gallantly to her defense. "Damn it all," he said, "you're about to make Joanna cry." With that he drew back his foot and kicked Jack on the shin with all his might. There was a dull thud. A stunned pause. Then "Ow! Ow! Ow!" Toby clutched his toes, poorly protected in soft leather, and began to hop about in agony. His ex-

pression changed so rapidly back and forth from
pain to astonishment that in spite of the fact that
no rescued maiden had ever mocked St. George
Joanna giggled hysterically. And to her surprise
Jack began to grin. "Serves you right," he said.

"It does not! You deserved to be kicked! And you
shouldn't always be so mean to Joanna," Toby
sobbed. "And you should have told me you were
like that, too."

"Like what?" Jack's eyes grew hard, all humor
drained from their expression.

"Like Wellington," Toby said. "Not the d-dog, the
m-man I mean. Of course, I knew that he was
made of iron. But no one told me his officers were
too. You should have said as much before I kicked
you."

"Dear God—the 'Iron Duke,' of course." Jack
choked and the tears streamed down Joanna's face
in earnest now but this time from suppressing
laughter.

"Let Emma look at your foot," she said to Toby as
soon as she could safely talk. "Maybe you should
soak it in cool water. And if there's room left inside
you after all those buns you ate, have her give you
a nuncheon too."

He left then, shooting back a dirty look which
now included both his relatives as he slammed the
door behind him.

Jack sat down again. "The Iron Duke! My God,
the things that go through children's heads."

"You really must tell him," Joanna said abruptly,
as all the humor of the situation vanished. "And
Addie too."

"No."

"Suit yourself, but I think you're underestimat-
ing them. But if you still insist on being stubborn,

112

at least your guilty secret's safe with Major Russell. I warned him not to speak of it."

"Oh, you did," Jack glowered. "I must say that you and Russell wasted no time in dealing on intimate terms together."

"You quite mistake the matter. There's nothing intimate about Molland's pastry cook shop, as you well know. The major merely inquired about your health—friends do such things, you may recall—and I stopped him from becoming explicit in front of Toby, that's all."

"All?" Jack sneered. "Evidently not. There must have been a great deal more to your meeting than you're saying since he's to call for you tomorrow. You must have quite bowled the poor widgeon over."

"Think whatever you like, then," she said, turning on her heel to leave and closing the door behind her with slightly less force than Toby had employed.

Joanna was halfway up the stairs before it occurred to her that what she had just done was typical. She could never best another in anything, not even in venting pent-up rage. As a statement, she felt her door slam had been most revealing.

Try that again, her demon muttered and she marched back down the stairs, opened the door wide, then slammed it with all her might. She could imagine that the very books came tumbling off the shelves.

An astonished Banks came flying into the hall to see what was amiss. "It's all right, Banks," she assured him gravely. "I got it right this time." And she walked sedately past him, then ran swiftly up the stairs.

113

Chapter Eleven

JACK'S RECEPTION OF Major Russell next morning was decidedly cool. The major in his turn had seemed delighted to see Jack and was about to grab his old comrade-in-arms and indulge in a bout of masculine backslapping when he was forestalled with a formal handshake. Although the major seemed nonplussed by this chilly greeting, he carried it off well by acknowledging his introduction to Addie and Godwin most cordially. And unknowingly he complied with Jack's wishes in the matter by inviting them all on the expedition to Sydney Gardens. But Addie and Jack were preengaged to try out the new rig Captain Rees had purchased and though Godwin's resolution wavered for just a moment, his pride prevented him from accompanying his sister and his pupil on an outing. Joanna urged him as much as she dared to, and even Toby said, "Do come. It will be famous, you'll see," but he mumbled some excuse about meeting a lady in the Pump Room that Joanna suspected he invented for Jack and Addie's sake.

She was distressed about her brother. He obviously was taking Miss Pelham's defection hard. Nor was he much more pleased with Addie's interest in Captain Rees. Joanna had heard him call the captain a "loose screw" to Addie's face and say that on the whole he thought she might fare better with

Bert the groom. His sister could have told him that his tactics were all wrong, that his set-down would simply enhance the captain in Addie's stubborn eyes, but it would have been a waste of breath. Their family seemed a hopeless tangle of cross purposes and there was nothing she or anybody else could do about it.

In spite of their shaky start, Toby, Wellington, the major, and Joanna had a most delightful morning. The weather had gone fine again after the intermittent drizzle the day before and there was nothing to prevent Toby and Wellington from dashing through the maze to their hearts' content. Their doing so gave Major Russell a chance to speak privately to Lady Welbourne.

"Jack seems much changed," he said abruptly. "From the way he greeted me, you might have thought us strangers. I assure you, I didn't invent the story of our friendship in order to insinuate myself into your company"—his gray eyes smiled into Joanna's—"though I might have done had I deemed it necessary. But truly, we were very close. I must admit I was taken aback by what I could only conclude was his obvious displeasure in seeing me."

Joanna, who had hoped to avoid the subject, looked uncomfortable. "Indeed, Major, you should not refine too much upon Jack's attitude. I fear his displeasure was for me."

He seemed astonished. "Surely he cannot object to your seeing other men? You are so young to be a widow. And your husband has been dead for more than a year. What could be more proper? Besides," he added, "though Jack was not one to discuss his personal affairs, I gained the impression that he was not so fond of his cousin as to want to keep his memory ever green."

"No, he was not fond of Gerald," she answered in

a restrained manner. "Or of anything belonging to his cousin."

"I see," the major answered, although his rather puzzled look belied the words. Just then Toby and Wellington joined them, and Joanna was thankful to be able to let the subject rest.

When they returned home some two hours later, she sent Toby in search of Emma to take him in charge awhile. She hoped for some time alone— perhaps in reading the latest horrid mystery that she'd had Godwin fetch her from the circulating library. But she was waylaid in the hallway by Jack's man Dawson, who was looking much perturbed.

"Beg pardon, ma'am," he said, "but I wish you'd have a word with Major Welbourne."

"Oh? I thought he'd gone out riding with Miss Sadler and Miss Pelham. Are they back already?"

"No, ma'am. The major begged off going. Said 'twas an urgent business matter that kept him home. But the truth is, he wasn't up to it. So I was wondering if your ladyship could persuade the major to send for a doctor. His leg's that bad that I'm afraid it may become putrid if it's not seen to. But he won't listen to a word I say, and since you're the only other one that knows the true state of things, and since he sets great store by your opinion—"

She had to laugh at that. "Dawson, I fear you much mistake the matter. He's more apt to do the exact opposite of anything I say. But really his attitude toward his injury is beyond belief! So if you think I should, I will beard the lion in his den. But you had best be prepared to rescue me."

Joanna sounded more courageous than she was feeling as she knocked upon Jack's door, softly at first and then with more authority.

"Who is it?" The growl was not encouraging.

"Joanna."

"Go away."

"No, Jack. I'm coming in." And forthwith she did so.

"Damn you, woman, have you never heard of modesty?" He snatched the coverlet to cover the lower part of his body as she entered but not quickly enough for her to fail to see that modesty was not the issue. Though he was shirtless, he wore his trowsers. It was the injury he sought to hide.

"Yes, I've heard of modesty. In fact you usually accuse me of possessing an excess of it. But at the moment modesty has nothing to say to anything. I want to see that leg."

"Like hell!"

"Like hell or like anything else," Joanna answered mildly. "Whether you like it or not, I am your cousin," she rather strangled on the word, "and I do not intend to let you do yourself irreparable harm through an excess of pride. So I want to see that leg. Then we can decide what's best to be done about it." She moved purposefully toward the bed.

"Joanna, I'm warning you. If you lay a hand on that counterpane, I'll break your arm."

She didn't doubt he meant it, but she reached for the cover anyway. His hand clamped like a vise upon her wrist. "I warned you," he said through clinched teeth. She reached out with the other hand, but he was quicker. He grabbed it too and squeezed while she did her best to bear the pain and give him stare for stare.

"We both know you can hurt me, Jack," Joanna said as calmly as she could, "but what's it in aid of? I intend to help you. You can, of course, break both my wrists and stop me."

"Goddamn you, Joanna Carrothers." For a moment she thought he would break her arms, he was

117

so enraged, but instead he gave her wrists a sudden yank that jerked her down on top of him. His arms crushed her to his bare chest as she tried to struggle upright. And then he kissed her—a bruising, punishing, rape of a kiss from an angry stranger. This was no lovemaking, for there was no love in it, no echo of the tenderness of their youth. But there was passion and to spare—a passion that it humiliated her to share since all his sprang from hate.

He finally released her and lay back against the pillows, breathing hard but smiling sardonically. Joanna sat for a moment shaken and gasping for breath. Then she slapped him hard across his mocking face.

"Just what have you proven—that you're still a man? I never doubted it."

"Oh, more than that, I think. I've also proven that you're something of a trollop."

Her face flamed but she kept her eyes steady on his face. "Well then. Now all that's out of your system, I'd like to finish what I set out to do." This time he didn't stop her as she sat down beside him and turned back the counterpane. He had pulled up his trowser leg to expose the stump. Joanna gasped at the sight of it.

"You're not as stalwart as you thought," Jack said sarcastically. "An amputation's not pretty, is it?"

"This one isn't certainly," she snapped at him. "You stubborn, vain, mutton-headed male! How could you do this to yourself?"

"You quite mistake the matter. The Frenchies did it."

"They merely shot it off," she retorted, full of fury at his senseless pride. "But you're the one who has not allowed it to heal properly. You've rubbed it raw

118

wearing that leg constantly. Not even allowing yourself to limp. Of all the stupid vanity—why, being stretched out on a rack couldn't hurt as much as this must have done." Her eyes filled with angry tears. "You've never had any sense at all, Coppy. It's like letting Gerald beat you half to death when you were Toby's size rather than say "enough." But I'll not stand for it. I'm sending Dawson right now to fetch a doctor and I plan to tell the family too. I'll ask them to keep it to themselves, if you prefer it that way. No outsider need know about it. But at least go about the house on crutches and give this a chance to heal. You're insane to have abused it so. Why, even when my Aunt Caroline got false teeth she was only able to wear them an hour or so at first until the gums toughened up properly."

Suddenly Jack's shoulders began to shake. She saw he was laughing helplessly. "Oh God, Joanna. I've had my whole damn leg blown away and you insist on acting as though I'd merely had my teeth drawn."

"Well, there is a parallel," she said, but not with much conviction.

"Do you think so? Well, I beg to differ. When a tooth's gone, it's gone. But would you believe that the leg that isn't even there hurts like bloody hell from the toes on up? I've even reached down to rub the thing and there's nothing there to rub."

She gazed at him with compassion. "Oh, Coppy."

"I've asked you not to call me that, and you've done it twice." His voice was cold again. He lay back on the pillows and closed his eyes. "But go on, send for the doctor if you wish." She got up and started for the door. "Joanna." She paused. "Don't tell the others, though." She started to protest, but the sight of his strained face with the beads of perspiration on his forehead changed her mind.

119

"Very well, if that's your wish," she said and went out the door.

Joanna consulted with a relieved Dawson, who went immediately to fetch a doctor. That gentleman, after spending some time alone with Jack, confirmed her own diagnosis that the leg needed rest and more time to heal. He left some bascilium powder that he felt should speed the process significantly, and Dawson went to work contriving some extra padding that should make the artificial limb more comfortable.

But to Joanna's surprise and considerable annoyance Jack appeared that night at dinner. They were all present, including Toby, though Addie and Godwin were going to the theater later on.

Jack avoided Joanna's glare of disapproval at his wearing the artificial limb again so soon. But perhaps the powders were working well, she thought hopefully. Then she noticed that he drank more heavily of the port than normally, to deaden the pain, she feared.

Despite whatever Jack might have suffered privately, dinner passed more pleasantly than did their usual meals. Toby was full of descriptions of his maze adventures, and Addie was excited over the play she and Godwin were going to see. Miss Newcomb had invited them all to join her in her box, but Joanna had begged off. Needless to say, she did not give her real excuse, that she disliked watching Miss Pelham set her cap for Jack. But then he too had been forced to send a note around. His excuse, she felt sure, was as false as hers. Wild horses would not make him admit his leg was paining him.

One member of the theater party was obviously not depressed by his defection. At least Joanna suspected that much of Godwin's high spirits resulted from the prospect of being in Miss Pelham's company without his rival. The tutor seemed quite lighthearted as he teased Addie about being more interested in the members of the *ton* she hoped to see than in the drama to be performed upon the stage.

"Well, why not? We can't all be scholars, for heaven's sake," she countered, but Joanna noted that she smiled up at Godwin engagingly.

At the end of the meal, before Addie and Godwin could excuse themselves, Jack cleared his throat for his family's attention. "I want to say—that is, Joanna feels that I should tell you something." He faltered a bit, as if hardly knowing how to proceed. "The fact is," he took a deep breath and forged ahead, "I really hadn't wanted to mention this. I hated the idea of the fuss it could cause—and being treated differently from the way I was accustomed to and all. But the fact is ... I caught a canon ball at Waterloo. My knee was shattered—and they had to amputate my leg. I wear a wooden one. But the damn thing has been giving me fits and the doctor says I must stay off it for a while. So I'll be on crutches around the house. I wanted to warn you though. So you'd not be too shocked to see me suddenly appear with an empty trowser leg flapping in the breeze." He stopped while three stricken faces stared at him, stunned to silence.

Toby, naturally, recovered first. "Oh, I say, was that the one I kicked?"

"Yes," his uncle answered.

"It's not made of iron then?"

"No, wood."

"Could I see it?" Toby's eyes suddenly sparkled with excitement.

"Oh, God, Toby," Jack answered, exasperated. "I suppose you can. But I'm telling you right now, I'm

121

not going to be the local freak show. So not a word to anybody, promise?" Toby nodded solemnly. "And I'd appreciate it if you two would not mention it as well." Addie and Godwin also nodded, their faces still reflecting enough distress to make Jack wince, but he plowed right on. "All right, Toby, you little ghoul. This is what a wooden leg looks like. And while'they all gathered round him, he stood up and raised his well-cut trowser leg and exposed the wooden limb that rose above the gleaming Hoby boot.

"Satisfied?" he said to Toby.

"Oh, I say, that's really a bang-up job," his nephew answered. "But can I see it when you take it off? I mean, how it works and all?"

"Yes," his uncle sighed.

"It's certainly well carved." Addie found her voice to blurt. "I mean, it's so well shaped and all. Does it match the other?" She immediately went pink at the impropriety.

"Quite well enough," Jack answered. "Do you wish to see it too and make comparisons?"

"Of course not." But she giggled and he grinned back.

Joanna suddenly relaxed.

"Do you have a name for it?" Toby inquired.

"Good God, no!"

"Lord Uxbridge calls his Old Timbertoes."

"I tell you right now, Toby, if you give this leg of mine a name, I'll break both of yours."

"What did they do with your other one?" They had resumed their seats, and Toby had his mouth crammed full of sweet.

"I haven't the slightest notion," Jack answered with distaste.

"You should have asked."

"I'm sorry, Toby. Do forgive the oversight, but I

didn't think of it at the time. I rather had other things on my mind."

"It must have been ghastly for you," Godwin blurted, then turned red, knowing how Jack would hate his sympathy.

Joanna held her breath, but Jack hesitated a moment and then said, "Yes, it was rather, thank you," and the crisis passed.

"But do you think they buried it?"

"I don't know, Toby. Probably. Now could we change the subject?"

"Do you think you could send for it?"

They all looked at him, appalled. "What a perfectly revolting idea," Jack said.

"It is not! I'm just thinking of you, you know. I mean, it should be buried back in Hampshire in the churchyard where you will be. So that when all the bones rise on Judgment Day you won't be legless. I don't believe it could ever find its way back on its own all the way from Belgium. You really should send for it now."

Godwin choked and sent a fine spray of wine all over the tablecloth. Addie went into spasms by his side. Joanna joined in too. She couldn't help it. Even Jack had to laugh helplessly while Toby looked disgusted at the reaction and went on stolidly eating apple snow.

"You were right again, Joanna." Jack looked down the long table toward her. "Here I was concerned about an excess of cloying sympathy from my family and my leg has turned into a bigger comedy routine than a play by Sheridan. I should have been prepared instead for heartless callousness."

"Oh, we are sorry, Uncle Jack. Truly we are," Addie giggled. "It's just that Toby's such a w-wet goose. And the images he conjures up! Can't you just hear the final trump sound forth—and see

123

your leg rising up at Waterloo while inquiring the best route back home to England?" And she fell into the whoops again with Godwin and Joanna following.

"Oh, God," Jack moaned and poured himself more port. "I really don't see how I can put up with much more of this. Exile is too damned good for Bonaparte."

Chapter Twelve

THEIR MISPLACED, NERVOUS gaiety was doomed to be short-lived. Instead of the treat they'd looked forward to, Addie and Godwin found the theater party decidedly flat, for Felicia did not come. Joanna heard all about it over breakfast. Jack was keeping to his room, so the disappointed pair felt free to let fly at one another.

"You are a complete peagoose if you believe she had the headache," Addie opened fire.

"Well, I do believe it," Godwin spit back.

"Females like Miss Pelham who drive their own phaetons and dress up like page boys and jump over the furniture at assemblies do not have the headache!" Addie retorted, cataloging some of the more shocking episodes attributed by the gossips to Miss Pelham.

"Those are a damned pack of Banbury Tales," Godwin said furiously, "and you would not repeat them if you were not jealous!"

"Of you?" Addie's voice dripped scorn.

"Of Miss Pelham. You long to be a Nonpareil like her. But she's decidedly above your touch."

"And yours too. Admit it! You know perfectly well that the only reason she had her famous headache and abandoned us to Miss Newcomb, who knows not one more soul in Bath than we do, was because Uncle Jack cried off. Admit it!"

"You only say that because you do not like her."

"And I do not like her for that very reason," Addie replied confusedly.

"And what's more your nose is out of joint because the so-called captain never showed up either. Which goes to show that his interest is in Felicia and not in you." Godwin won the day with that Parthian shot, but since the point he made was as distressing to him as it was to Addie, the victory was a hollow one.

They saw very little of Jack the next few days. He kept to his room and the library, having his meals brought on a tray. Joanna assumed he was giving his leg a rest from the artificial one, but since he was seated behind his desk during the only conversation she had with him, she really wasn't sure. He called to her as she passed the library.

"May I see you a moment, Joanna?" He was very stiff and formal. She walked in and stood waiting, while he seemed to search for words. "I realize an apology for my conduct the other day is overdue," he said abruptly. "I do beg your pardon for it. I behaved most ungentlemanly—and then said things I should not have said."

"Like calling me a trollop?" Joanna answered coolly. She knew she should not have brought it up again, but his tone and manner seemed so far removed from true repentance that she was angered rather than mollified by his apology.

"Yes," he answered, his dark eyes hard. "I should not have said that. Or have kissed you. Needless to say, I'll not repeat my conduct."

"Your apology is accepted then." He didn't miss the irony of her tone.

"I'll not crawl to you, Joanna. I've admitted my wrong and that's as far as I care to go."

"It's even farther than was necessary; I had already forgotten the incident," she answered, feeling that she was, after all, acting rather childishly. Jack's apology might not have been exactly heartfelt, but it had cost him quite a bit to make it. She tried for a more pleasant tone. "Addie and I are going to the Pump Room. Is there any errand we might run for you?"

"No, just give my best to Charlie when you see him," he said nastily.

So much for pleasantness, Joanna thought. "If I see him, I most surely will," she answered, going out.

It was impossible for Addie to remain in the dumps for long. The attention she received from the young beaux gathered in the Pump Room cheered her immensely. And that evening as the family sat drinking tea in the gold drawing room she was full of plans for the dress ball to be held in the Upper Assembly Rooms the following Monday night. Her whole future seemed to hang upon whether she wore the spotted or the tamboured muslin. "You are going with us, are you not?" She ceased her wardrobe planning to direct the question to her uncle, who had come out of his solitary state to join them.

"No," he answered.

"Whyever not? You can't be in Bath for the Season and not attend the balls. Even if you can't dance, there's always the card room. Or you can simply mingle with the *ton* and engage in flirts— though it's beyond me why you should not participate in the country dances," she rattled on. "Mostly one just stands and converses with one's partner and you move so well that I'm sure you will manage nicely when it comes your turn to be top couple. If you like, Joanna or I will stand up with you at first till you get over feeling ill at ease," she finished up ingenuously.

"Thank you." Addie entirely missed the irony in his voice that caused her aunt to look uncomfortable. "But despite your generosity in partnering me, I think I shall decline. The truth is, I absolutely refuse to be seen in knee smalls."

"Oh." Addie was momentarily dampened by the strict rule of dress set by Beau Nash in the first half of the eighteenth century and relaxed but little in the present day. It was easy to see why Jack was loath to wear the required knee britches and silk hose. There would be no hiding his infirmity, despite the skillful construction of his artificial limb. "I know!" Addie suddenly exclaimed with the same enthusiasm that Archimedes must have shown when he shouted out "Eureka!" "You can go in uniform. There are sure to be others there. Why, I expect that Major Russell will wear his."

"Wouldn't it appear a bit strange now that I've sold out?" Jack answered, but it was obvious he was mulling over the suggestion.

"Not a bit of it." Addie pressed her advantage. "No one will refine the least upon it. But if they did, they'd only think you had not got around to having evening clothes made yet. Which is true, of course."

Jack was weakening fast, but he raised a last objection. "I doubt Dawson brought my uniform along. It certainly would have been an odd thing for him to do."

But when Addie dispatched Toby at once to inquire about it, it seemed that the redoubtable Dawson had indeed fetched Jack's dress uniform.

"It's settled then," Addie said with smug satisfaction. "We shall all be going to the ball."

"I would not go if you paid me to," her little

brother said, obviously disliking her careless use of "all." "I should hate it above all things. I can understand why silly females want to dance. But why men should do such a ramshackle thing is wonderful."

"Toby, as always your wisdom exceeds your years," Jack said. "Dancing is rather a ramshackle pursuit when one stops to consider. I therefore shall content myself with the heady pleasure of cards—no hazard is allowed, I believe, so I shall not lose what's left of the family fortune. And if that excitement should begin to pall, I shall quiz the *ton*, as Addie has suggested. Who knows, perhaps a whole new crop of eligibles may have arrived in Bath."

On the following Monday night Joanna, Adelaide, and Godwin collected in the hall to await the chairs that would carry them to the Assembly Rooms. Addie looked radiant, Joanna thought with pride. The girl had settled on the tamboured frock—white, trimmed with palest blue that suited her dark hair, light eyes, and tender years. Joanna wore a more mature ensemble of figured lace over a satin underdress of dusky rose, quite her favorite color. The fact that Jack had used to like it too had had no bearing, she told herself, upon her choice. Godwin was looking suddenly quite grown-up, though a bit self-conscious, in his white knee breeches and black long-tailed coat. Joanna caught a whiff of lavender water as he passed her.

Only the most churlish, Joanna thought, would have denied that the three of them made an attractive trio, that is, until they were quite eclipsed by Jack's military splendor. He fairly glittered. His close-fitting coat was topped with gold epaulets. A profusion of gold braid adorned a collar so

129

high that a snowy neckcloth was barely seen. More braid ran riot across his chest. Gold stripes trimmed the legs of his neatly tapered but unrevealing trowsers.

"Oh, you look beautiful," Addie had gasped when he joined them in the hall.

"My God, I hope not," had been his answer, but he'd looked pleased, Joanna noted, all the same.

Once they'd reached the Assembly Rooms, Jack deserted them. Godwin soon followed his example. Joanna was sure her brother was working his way through the crush looking for Miss Pelham. She could only hope this had not been Jack's immediate goal as well. She tried to dismiss them from her mind, however, as Mr. King, the Master of Ceremonies, appeared with a shy-looking partner whom he introduced to Addie.

Good manners should have prompted that young lady to look more pleased, though Joanna knew she longed to stand up first with Captain Rees, who was certain to be somewhere within the throng. But it would not have done to make excuses. Her aunt was glad to see her good nature reassert itself and cause her to set the young gentleman at ease as he led her into the set.

Miss Newcomb was beckoning from the chaperon's section. Joanna made her way toward her through the crowd and sat down beside her. "How lovely you look, my dear," Miss Newcomb said. "You even take the shine off Adelaide, which is an achievement, I can assure you. How nice to see you finally. I've been longing for a comfortable coze."

"Then you are going to be most out of charity with me, ma'am." They looked up to see Major Russell smiling down at them. "I've hacked my swordless way through the crush to ask Lady Welbourne to stand up with me."

He was not in uniform, as Addie had predicted, but in civilian evening clothes. Involuntarily Joanna glanced at his well-shaped legs clad in the required knee smalls and wondered if Jack's undoubted jealousy of his friend arose from the fact he'd survived Waterloo unscathed.

"Oh, I had not planned to dance." She smiled up at the major.

"Of course she shall dance," Miss Newcomb interposed. The major smiled his thanks to her quite charmingly, then took Joanna by the hand to join a set just forming for a country dance. They stood idly chatting for a moment, the major entertaining her with comments on this or that remarkable person in the hall, until both their eyes were drawn toward Jack, who stood with two other gentlemen near the exit to the card room. One was holding forth upon some topic while the other listened. But Jack's attention was all for the dancing couple, his face unguarded in its bitterness. Then he caught them looking at him and turned to face the speaker.

"He's in love with you," the major remarked offhand, the way someone mentions the likelihood of rain. "I should have known."

"Indeed, you quite mistake the matter. The truth is that he hates me."

"That's just as bad," was his reply. "If he merely disliked you, I'd call that encouraging. I've known Jack Welbourne for these many years and I've yet to best him in anything, but I intend to keep on trying. By the by—you don't pity him because of the leg by any chance?"

"Whatever can you mean? Of course, I'm sorry for it. But pity? One does not pity Jack."

"Good. I would not want him to have that unfair advantage."

The music had begun and kept her from replying, which was just as well since she was at a loss for words.

"I believe I can ask you to stand up with me twice," the major said at the conclusion of the set. "The roof should not cave in or Mr. King suffer palpitations—though if I were so rash as to solicit your hand for a third time, one or both of those things would be certain to occur."

She laughed and consented to be his partner once again. As they stood waiting for the set to form, Joanna put the fan she carried to good use, for the crowded dance floor had become quite warm. She gazed around and noted with mixed feelings that Addie had been claimed by Captain Rees. She was glowing up at him in a way she could not be pleased to see in spite of wishing her to enjoy the ball.

Afterward, when Joanna again took a seat beside Miss Newcomb, she saw that Addie was to be the captain's partner a second time. Miss Newcomb saw the direction of her gaze and read her thoughts. "I can't think either that he's a suitable companion for Addie and am quite out of charity with Felicia for promoting it." She frowned. "But then I fear I am out of charity with Felicia on most things. She is my dear brother's only child, but that cannot blind me to her faults. She is, I fear, a shocking flirt and is bound to hurt your brother—if indeed she has not already done so. Now Jack is quite another matter. He's no 'green 'un to be gulled by her' if you'll excuse my shocking choice of words. Felicia has had her influence even upon me, you see." She smiled but then turned serious once again. "Indeed, the harm may be quite the other way around. She may be the victim this time. For I suspect she really cares for Jack. But I cannot tell whether he is seriously interested in her or not. Can you?"

"No," Joanna answered, rather repressively perhaps, for her friend threw her a shrewd look.

"Of course I had hoped that you and he—"

She left the statement in the air and Joanna replied quickly, "There is no question of anything like that."

"Well then perhaps he and Felicia might not be a bad match after all. Her fortune would put his estates to rights, and I do believe he'd be quite competent in keeping her in line. My brother would be pleased, I'm sure," she sighed. "He's a very conventional man and Felicia has been a sore trial to him."

Joanna could well believe it. Felicia was a trial to most of her acquaintances, she thought uncharitably as she looked around for a glimpse of the Nonpareil. She had spied her earlier dancing with the poet but had not seen her for some time now. Nor had she seen Jack, a fact which did not help raise her spirits from the depths into which Miss Newcomb had unwittingly plunged them.

Just then her brother came to claim her hand. Godwin seemed so glum Joanna could only conclude that his dance with Felicia had somehow sunk his spirits. If so, he still directed all his ire toward Addie. "How could she be so shatterbrained as to encourage that Here-and-therein is more than I can see. The man's a coxcomb—and a gamester and a libertine as well from all I hear." Joanna followed his dark gaze to where Addie stood next to the wall using her fan flirtatiously while gazing up at Captain Rees. "She just refused to dance with me. Said she felt faint—of all the rappers I ever heard! Now look at her!"

"Well, she isn't dancing," Joanna said. But the observation did not seem to mollify him.

When the set was finished, Joanna steered them over to join Addie, who was now seated by herself. The captain, she said, had gone to fetch tea for her. It was now nine o'clock and the dancing would stop a bit while the dancers and musicians rested. Captain Rees soon rejoined them, the restorative for Addie in his hand. But he had been employed in other business.

"I say," he beamed, "I've persuaded the orchestra to play a waltz. Lady Millsaps," he referred to one of the Bath pillars of society, "actually condescended to back me up. 'Since Czar Alexander danced the waltz at Almack's,' she informed the orchestra leader in that haughty voice of hers, 'that dance has become unexceptional. Only the hopelessly Gothic could possibly object.' So, Miss Sadler," he bowed to Addie, "I hope you will do me the honor of waltzing with me."

"She'll do nothing of the sort," the poet growled.

"I beg your pardon?" Captain Rees picked up his quizzing glass to give Godwin an icy stare. Though a fop, Captain Rees was certainly no milksop, Joanna realized and felt more than a little frightened. Godwin's face reddened at his own impetuosity, but he stuck bravely to his guns.

"I m-mean to say," he paused to check his tendency to stammer when under stress, "what the czar did at Almack's has nothing to say to Addie's conduct here at Bath. You must know it would be improper for her to waltz with you. She's not even out yet officially."

"He's right, you know." A calm voice spoke behind them, nipping a certain quarrel in the bud and also halting the scathing set-down that Addie longed to hurl in Godwin's teeth. "It would be most improper

134

for my niece to dance the waltz with you, Captain Rees," Jack said. "So I advise you to seek another more suitable partner for it."

For a moment Rees's anger seemed merely transferred to a different target. But something in Jack's eyes made him shrug and capitulate. He bowed low to Joanna, smiling most charmingly. "Will you get me off the hook then, Lady Welbourne? Since I've started all this uproar about the shocking waltz, will you not take pity and partner me?"

The waltz music was beginning and two or three couples had ventured out onto the floor. "I advised you to look for a suitable partner, Rees," Jack said. "Lady Welbourne never behaves improperly."

Joanna had had her excuses on her lips. But Jack's words stung quite as much as they were intended to. "I should love to waltz," she answered, smiling at the captain and accepting his proffered hand. She had a moment of near sinful satisfaction as she saw the astonishment on the faces of her family when they left them standing there.

"Thank you for saving my face," the captain said.

"I'm not sure I have," she answered ruefully. "The truth is, I've never danced the waltz in public. Only with Addie and Godwin in our home and we were never sure that we had got it right."

The captain laughed and placed a hand upon Joanna's waist, an intimacy that might have put her to the blush had she not been quite determined not to let it. He guided her out among the dancers —the couples had swelled to six now—while the rest of the company gawked at them.

So skillful a partner was Captain Rees that Joanna soon forgot her self-consciousness in the lilt of the music and the grace and exhilaration of the movements. She quite enjoyed herself. But only for a moment. For while they whirled among the other waltzers, she spied Jack and Felicia upon the floor. What could he be thinking of, he couldn't possibly manage. These thoughts made her stumble, and she hastily begged her partner's pardon.

But Joanna had underestimated the skill of both of them. Due no doubt to his long sojourn on the continent, Jack was obviously no stranger to the waltz. He had always been a natural athlete and a skilled dancer. But no more so than his partner, it soon appeared. Theirs was a virtuoso exhibition, especially awesome to those who knew of Jack's handicap. His own movements were actually quite curtailed. But this was hardly noticeable. Rhythmically, unfalteringly, he led Felicia in an improvisation that gave her the starring role. For grace and beauty, Joanna reluctantly admitted to herself, Jack's partner rivaled the most professional opera dancer to be seen on any stage. When the music ended, the onlookers actually broke into applause. All the dancers then smiled and bowed as though they and the waltz shared in the tribute. But Joanna, for one, knew that the admiration all belonged—and rightly so—to Jack and the "odious" Miss Pelham.

Captain Rees escorted Joanna to a seat as far from the chaperon section as they could manage. She did not feel up to encountering the raised eyebrows of her elders there. Whether she should have danced at all in her widowed state, she felt was questionable, but to have been among the waltzers must have sunk her below redemption. She could imagine that poor Miss Newcomb was hard-pressed to defend both her niece and friend for their exhibitionism.

Oh well, she told herself. Her only real regret was that she allowed Jack to goad her into such alien conduct. She wished she had decided for herself, for actually it was time she did something slightly shocking. But when Captain Rees left her to claim his current partner, rather than outface the company, she took refuge behind three large young ladies who lacked partners but talked animatedly among themselves. She fanned vigorously, for her cheeks were hot, whether from exercise or embarrassment she could not say. After a bit she was joined by Addie, who looked a little green.

"Joanna, I'm not feeling at all the thing. Do you think we might get some air?"

"Of course." Joanna rose hastily before the heat and the excitement should prove to be the girl's complete undoing. She hurried to the cloakroom to get their wraps, and they slipped outside into the fresh air.

"Oh, that's better," Addie gasped as they stepped out into the cloudy night. "I don't know what came over me. I felt quite light-headed."

"Perhaps you should have eaten a bit before we came," Joanna chided.

"I was too excited. Besides, I'm determined to be thinner than Felicia Pelham before I'm through."

They had slipped out a side door and were walking slowly and silently around the building with Addie taking deep gulps of air as they progressed. Suddenly they stopped short and clutched at one another.

At first Joanna thought the shadow in the shrubbery was just one person, a footpad, perhaps, lurking to prey on helpless females. She had just sorted out a man and woman locked in an embrace when the clouds broke capriciously apart to let the moon shine through. Beside her Addie gasped. Felicia Pelham stood on tiptoe, her back to them, her arms clutching at Jack's shoulders while he and she kissed passionately. So oblivious was Felicia that

137

she heard neither their footsteps nor Addie's quick intake of breath. But Jack heard. Or else he had taken up kissing with his eyes wide open. He in no way betrayed the watchers' presence to his partner, though, for the kiss continued. But his eyes looked straight into Joanna's until she grabbed her niece's arm and they turned and fled. Even then it did not appear that Felicia Pelham regained consciousness.

Back in the cloakroom, where fortunately they were alone, Addie and Joanna could only stare at one another. Addie broke the silence.

"I hate her," she said viciously.

Since "amen" was the only thing that occurred to her aunt to say, she did not answer.

"She's no better than a—a—Cyprian," Adelaide railed on, using one of the more polite terms for a Lady of the Evening. "Anyone might have walked by and seen them. A whole parade in fact with fife and drum and she'd not have noticed." She giggled involuntarily at the notion and then quickly sobered up. "Poor Godwin," she said to Joanna's surprise. "Do you suppose it will hurt him very much?"

Godwin was furthest from Joanna's thoughts just then. "I don't know. Probably," she said.

"He's well rid of her. Do you think this means that they're engaged?"

"I've no idea."

"I hope not. I'd rather it be Uncle Jack than Godwin, I suppose, but why either one of them has to fall into her clutches is more than I can say. She may be rich as Croesus but what does that signify when you take into consideration how odious she is. I say—did she do it on purpose to entrap him?"

"I don't know what you mean."

"Kiss him in a public place where they were almost bound to be seen—so he'd have to offer for her, that's what."

"I think you quite mistake the matter. He no doubt chose the time and place."

Jack's niece snorted indelicately. "That shows how little you know about it," she said. "You can't have been looking properly if you think that. She was plastered against him like a mustard poultice and kissing him for all that she was worth. I don't think he was even helping. He looked bored to death, in fact."

"Perhaps he just doesn't like performing for an audience," Joanna answered dryly. "He had the disadvantage of being turned our way."

"Just the same—" The arrival of some other patrons cut short whatever Addie had planned to say, and Joanna left her there to search for Godwin. He was standing dejectedly against the wall and seemed more than happy to go home, though it was only ten o'clock and the ball would not finish until eleven. "Shall I find Jack and tell him that we're leaving?"

"Oh, no," his sister said too quickly, which caused him to look rather oddly at her.

Outside again, while Godwin went to find a chair, Joanna kept her eyes resolutely on the street, but Addie made no bones about looking all around. "They've gone," she stage-whispered just as Godwin rejoined them.

"Who's gone?" he asked.

"No one of importance," she answered. "Just someone we saw here before."

"Jack and Felicia, I'll bet a monkey," Godwin snarled.

It was a much gloomier party that arrived back at the Royal Crescent than the one that had left it a few hours earlier. Godwin didn't even bother to bid the ladies a good night, but went straight upstairs to his room.

"Men are so stupid," Addie exploded at his retreating back. "Now he'll be blue-deviled for days on her account. And it's all my fault."

"Your fault?" Joanna was astonished. "How could you be in any way to blame?"

"I talked Uncle Jack into going in the first place, didn't I? And told him to wear the uniform. How was I to know he'd look so dashing in it? I can hardly blame Felicia Pelham for making a complete cake out of herself and acting shamelessly. If he were not my uncle, I'd be in love with him myself."

It was a point of view that touched a sympathetic chord. For he was not Joanna's uncle. And from the tortures of jealousy she was experiencing, she had to know the truth. She was, in fact, still in love with him.

Chapter Thirteen

THE ONLY ONES who didn't look embarrassed when they met the next day were the guilty lovers. Miss Pelham and her aunt came to pay a morning call at the Royal Crescent after Miss Newcomb had drunk her daily round of Pump Room waters. They all gathered in the small sitting room, including Toby whom Joanna had allowed to stay since Miss Newcomb liked his company so much and Miss Pelham cared for it so little. Besides, Joanna needed him. For no matter what the social atmosphere, Toby could be counted upon to remain unself-conscious and at ease. She was grateful for his chatter as he described to a quite interested Miss Newcomb just how she might navigate the intricacies of the maze without being hedged in and lost forever.

Under cover of this distraction, Joanna stole a look at Felicia Pelham and Jack Welbourne, side by side upon a sofa. She was in love with him, there was no mistake. In marked contrast to Addie, Godwin, and herself, who vied with one another to seem the most blue-deviled, Felicia was radiant. And beautiful. Joanna sank even lower into her gloom. Addie and she were just being cattish about Felicia's unusual eyes. They made her face more interesting. It was not just her money that had attracted him. She was the sort of woman he had always most admired.

It was painful to acknowledge that Miss Pelham was the perfect mate for Jack. Wild and headstrong, the Londoner matched him on almost every level. If Felicia had been around when they were young, Joanna concluded glumly, he'd never have noticed Joanna at all. And now he never failed to make it clear at every opportunity that she was the type of conventional, spiritless woman he most despised.

Jack caught her covertly studying them and looked amused. Joanna, unaccountably, was put to the blush while he remained unabashed. In fact, he seemed to be enjoying her discomfort more than he did Felicia's nearness. *He makes a better enemy than a lover,* she thought with jealous satisfaction.

"Don't forget our excursion to Sham Castle." Felicia murmured the words for Jack's ears alone, but they came during a lull in Toby's recitation and so were clearly audible to everyone.

"But you promised to go with me!" The words, or their equivalent, were in duet. Toby's sentence was directed toward Jack and Godwin's to Felicia.

Jack chose to answer both of them. "There's no problem then. You two shall come along."

Nobody seemed pleased with this Solomonlike solution, Felicia least of all.

"Perhaps Toby and Godwin would prefer another time, since we've already made our plans to ride."

"I like riding above all things," Toby declared with a mutinous look that boded no good for Felicia's maneuvering.

"But we had planned to walk there." Godwin sounded very hurt and younger than Toby. Joanna would have kicked him for wearing his heart upon his sleeve could she have managed it unobtrusively.

"How shatterbrained of me. When we laid our plans, I fear I forgot you cannot ride." Felicia's tone was quite as false as his earlier poems had labeled her. "I beg your pardon for it. It's so wonderfully odd that a man cannot go on horseback that it simply slipped my mind."

Godwin's face turned red, then white by turns, while Addie fairly bristled. "Godwin not ride?" She entered the lists with an airy laugh. "Where did you get such an odd notion? Of course he rides. He's just too proud to make use of Uncle Jack's cattle, that's all. But when the Carrothers kept a stable, he rode all the time." Addie's eyes snapped so as she delivered this quelling fabrication that not even Felicia dared question it.

Godwin's expression changed from humiliation to astonishment at this unexpected championship. Miss Newcomb looked thoughtful and Jack even more amused. Joanna tried to keep her face expressionless. But Toby worried her. His eyes had grown big as saucers at his sister's sudden declaration, and Joanna was sure he was going to take her to task for such an out-and-out untruth. Indeed, his mouth was opening to utter when Banks providentially appeared. "Major Russell and Captain Rees," he said, and in the ensuing bustle of greetings and tea pourings the sticky subject of Godwin's equestrian skill was mercifully forgotten.

It was Felicia who invited the newcomers, along with Joanna and Adelaide, on the excursion to Sham Castle. Joanna could only guess at her motive. Perhaps she was annoyed with Jack for enlarging the party beyond a cozy twosome and wanted to get back at him by flinging Captain Rees at Addie's head. Or perhaps she merely wished to avoid a lecture from Miss Newcomb on the impropriety of a lone female junketing off unchaperoned with two men and a little boy. At any rate it soon was settled—all eight of them would take a picnic

143

lunch and ride forth day after next to see that strange structure and explore the countryside around it.

The door had barely closed behind the guests when Toby pointed an accusing finger at Adelaide. "You told a whisker!"

"Oh, do be quiet!" his sister said and burst into tears.

Toby looked aghast. "I say, Addie, I didn't mean to make you cry. I don't blame you one little bit. In fact I was going to say that Godwin was a regular goer myself, 'pon my soul I was; I just didn't get the chance. But I didn't half like what that Miss Pelham said about his not knowing how to ride. And she told a bigger whisker than you did when she said she'd forgot she promised to see Sham Castle on foot with him. I don't see why she doesn't just pick on somebody like Captain Rees anyhow and leave Godwin and Uncle Jack alone. Captain Rees can walk and ride both—and he needs her money just as much as they do."

Toby's happy solution to their family's romantic rivalry was one that Joanna heartily, if silently, applauded. But it seemed to have no effect on the two male principals. Jack's only comment was to excuse himself. As for her brother, he was sunk into a deep study of some kind and hardly noticed the other's exit. Addie sniffed a few more times, dabbed at her eyes with a wisp of lace, then said, "Godwin, I could t-teach you to ride, you know. Enough to get by on."

"No, thank you," he answered stiffly.

"How like you!" Addie blazed. "To simply lie down and be walked over. If you actually want that odious female, then put up a fight for her. Don't just hand her over to Uncle Jack. You're as good a man as he is any day, so act like one."

"I didn't say I was going to do nothing," Godwin

144

answered. "I just can't see you teaching me to ride, that's all. You'd be bound to fly up into the boughs when I wasn't a bruiser in the first five minutes. So I think I'll go right now to Mr. Dash's riding school in Montpelier Row. Would you like to come along?"

"I should like it above all things."

"Do you promise to keep quiet and let them do all the instructing?"

"Can I come too?" Toby pleaded eagerly.

"Why not," Godwin said with an air of resignation. "If I'm to make a fool of myself on the Sham Castle trip, I might as well start getting used to it right off. Come along, you little horse-riding monster. But if I land on my backside and you and Addie say one word, I shall throttle both of you."

"I won't laugh, I promise," Toby answered solemnly. "No matter how big a gudgeon you appear."

Addie giggled and Godwin groaned. "Here begins my martyrdom," he said as they bade his sister good-bye. But she noticed he looked remarkably cheerful all the same.

On the way to her bedchamber Joanna passed Jack in the upstairs hall. It was, as always, difficult for her to tell whether the harsh lines of his face and the aloofness of his gaze were brought on by the effort to disguise his pain or from his dislike of meeting her. The latter, she concluded since this was their first time alone since she'd been a shocked witness of the kiss. To cover her own awkwardness she inquired with prim politeness, "How does your leg feel, Jack?"

"Which one, Joanna?"

She didn't rise to his bait, so he continued. "One feels like wood, thank you, and the other like ordinary flesh. It's the one buried and rotten some place that still hurts like hell."

Joanna wheeled on him. "Stop it!" she said. "There's no point any more to what you're doing."

"What am I doing? I merely honestly answered a question that you had asked to cover what you evidently consider an awkward meeting."

"All meetings with you are awkward," she retorted.

"Only for you. Perhaps your conscience hurts."

She chose to misunderstand him. "My conscience need not trouble me about last night. I assure you that Addie and I were not spying. You should choose less public places to make love."

He shrugged. "No doubt. But circumstances have a way of dictating that sort of thing. Everyone's not as calculating in their love life as you, Joanna."

He laughed softly as she turned without a further word and left him.

Thursday morning dawned bright and clear in spite of Joanna's prayers for rain.

"We look ready for a Cavalry charge, would you not say so, Welbourne?" Major Russell, like Joanna two days before, was making idle conversation to cover awkwardness. The party had gathered in the Circus. A cool nod had been Jack's only greeting before the major asked his fatuous question.

Jack took a moment to calm his impatient stallion; then he looked them over. His sardonic gaze traveled slowly from a jubilant Toby perched like a little monkey on a full-sized horse, to Godwin seated uneasily on his rented mount, to Addie nervously watching him, to Felicia wearing the latest London crack in riding habits and looking with ill-disguised contempt at Joanna's country clothes, and finally came to rest on Captain Rees who was just joining them ten minutes late, time necessary no doubt to achieve his sartorial splendor which

146

featured a lilac riding cape with matching hat and boot tops.

"Your memory of Cavalry charges and mine seem to be at variance," Jack finally deigned to answer.

Major Russell looked at Joanna and shrugged, a gesture that Jack, she noted, did not fail to see.

"Well, tally ho!" Captain Rees called out cheerfully. "Come set the pace with me, Miss Sadler. We'll make up for the time I've cost you and leave these slow-tops to eat our dust."

Addie, however, was loath to abandon her role as Godwin's mother hen. She gave the poet an anxious look. He scowled resentfully. Her answering head toss had a "go to the devil" quality about it as she kicked her mare with her riding boot and moved out to follow the captain's lead.

Joanna, too, was anxious about Godwin in this company of bruising riders. Two cavalrymen and a self-styled fop, who added horse racing to the list of idle pursuits, made rough comparison for a rank beginner. But two full days of instruction had given Godwin a certain competency as well as a host of aches and pains. He'd been sensibly mounted too, his sister noted. His horse was no fire-breathing blood such as the one Jack was riding, but it was certainly no hack. A far more seasoned rider would not have been put to the blush by it. Joanna watched as he quickly moved to Felicia's side and saw that he handled himself quite creditably. Since it made sense to ride no more than two abreast, Jack fell back with Toby, which delighted that young man but put Felicia out of humor. She chose to vent her spleen upon poor Godwin, digging her heel viciously into her horse's flank and breaking into a gallop, ill-suited both for a novice rider to imitate and for the crowded streets. "I for one have no intention to eating dust," she cried back over her shoulder.

In spite of Addie's stirring declaration of Godwin's skill two days before, Joanna felt sure that Felicia knew the true state of his experience with horses and intended to show him up for the slow-top she expected him to be. But he struck out gamely after her while his sister held her breath and prayed he'd neither break his own neck nor run down some hapless pedestrian in the street.

"Huzzah!" Toby spurred after them with a gleeful shout, but Jack quickly ran him down and grabbed his rein. "Save that for the countryside or go back home," he answered his nephew's outraged protest. "We've unleashed enough fools already without you going neck-or-nothing through the town."

"Shall I tell Miss Pelham you just called her a fool?" Toby glared.

"If it will make you happy," Jack answered coolly and rode on ahead.

Once they'd left Bath behind, the riding party regained at least a semblance of good nature. Felicia recovered from her pet and chattered charmingly at Godwin, whether for his benefit or Jack's, Joanna could not help but wonder. But if Godwin was indeed the target, the siren's spell was slipping, his sister thought. The poet seemed less dazzled by Felicia's flirts than proud of his equestrian skills in keeping pace with her.

"I do believe the scales are falling from his eyes," the major murmured as he and Joanna drew near the spot where the two leaders waited for them. The captain and Addie had prudently fallen behind. "And you alarmed yourself for nothing. Your brother handled his horse like a veteran. I've had cavalrymen under me not half so skilled."

"Really, Major, that's coming it a bit strong." She

smiled up at him. "But Godwin does do remarkably well, does he not?"

"Remarkably well indeed," he answered solemnly, his eyes smiling back at her.

"It would be most unhandsome if you were teasing me. But truly, Major, if Godwin rides as well as you'd lead me to believe, how did you come to suspect that he's only a beginner?"

"I could say from your and Addie's mother-hen concern, but the truth is, Toby told me."

"I might have known," she groaned. "With Toby around no skeletons are safe in the family cupboard."

"None at all," he answered gravely, his eyes holding hers as she felt her face grow hot.

"Come on, you slow-tops," Toby shouted back at them. Thankful for the distraction, Joanna urged her horse into a canter. She and the major joined the others just as Sham Castle came into view.

From a distance the castle looked ancient and crumbling, a Gothic ruin romantically crowning the hilltop, an awesome sight against the skyline to be seen for miles around. But the closer the party came, the more the illusion lessened, just as a stage castle might lose its mystique if one penetrated beyond the footlights and examined it too closely. For the castle, as its name implied, truly was a sham. Built for Ralph Allen of Prior Park, its only function had been to improve the view, adding a touch of romance to the dull, bare hilltop. It was a frontage with nothing at all behind. An empty mask with battlements like pasteboard turrets in a play and crossbow slits through which no arrows had ever flown.

"There must be a moral somewhere in all of this," Captain Rees remarked as he gazed upward at the mock ediface, "but I'm dashed if I can come up with it."

"I'm astonished that you cannot," Godwin muttered a bit too audibly as he looked at Rees's own picturesque facade. For just a moment something ugly showed within the Corinthian's eyes, but then he merely smiled. "Suppose you write a sonnet and point it out for me—Poet."

But Felicia Pelham had had enough of castle gazing. "You said we were like the Cavalry," she called to Major Russell. "I vote that we map out our campaign and storm this castle."

"What a bang-up idea!" Toby bounced up and down upon his saddle and for the first time ever looked at Miss Pelham with something like approval. "We can all be Knights Templar and Sham Castle will be a Saracen stronghold."

Joanna had expected some sort of set-down from Jack, at least, but the eagerness on Toby's face was suddenly infectious, and they were all children once again. Without a word they grouped their horses and glared upward toward the foe.

"Lead the charge then, Toby," Jack called out.

"Should I?" Toby's eyes were sparkling. "But that would not be quite the thing, would it, Uncle Jack, with you and Major Russell here? I mean to say, you both have been at Waterloo and all sorts of other charges and know exactly how it's done."

"There's nothing to it that you can't handle, Toby," Major Russell assured him solemnly. "Just brandish your pretend sword for all you're worth and do a prodigious lot of yelling. We'll all join in."

"And if you see any poltroons—me, for example—sneaking toward the rear to catch the first ship back to England," Captain Rees chimed in, "use the flat of your sword upon them."

"Oh, you won't do that," Toby answered him quite

150

seriously. "You're Templars, don't you know. By the way—what should a Knight Templar shout?"

"How about 'Storm the Castle!'?" the major suggested and got a pained look for his colorless battle cry.

"Well then, 'For England and St. George!' seemed an all-purpose sort of rallying cry when I was your age," his uncle proffered.

"I'm sure the Knights Templar had their own special thing to say, but if no one knows it"— Toby looked pointedly at his tutor, who shrugged his shoulders in embarrassed ignorance—"I suppose Uncle Jack's cry will have to do. All right then. Is everybody ready to storm the battlements and destroy the Infidel?" Assuming a most martial attitude, Toby rose in his stirrups and raised his hand on high. "For England and St. George!" he whooped.

The others echoed him, "For England and St. George!" Then they charged pell-mell, racing one another to the top, laughing and screeching enough to confound an astonished foe. Once having gained the summit unchecked by the hail of imaginary arrows, they circled the castle several times, whooping more like American Indians than any Knights Templar Joanna ever read of.

"I'm hit!" Captain Rees yelled dramatically above the din. Since the marksmanship from the beleaguered castle seemed too much to cope with, Toby sounded a retreat—to regroup, of course—and they started down the hill again, as fast as their gallant steeds would take them. Addie and Joanna raced neck and neck, shouting to one another "Beware the arrows!" Suddenly Joanna's horse tripped and fell and she went pitching off above its head.

She did recall breaking her fall somewhat with her hands—fortunately no bones were also broken—but her head collided with a rock and stunned her momentarily. What happened immediately thereafter she learned from Addie later on. The girl vowed that it was quite the worst moment of her life, seeing Joanna stretched out pale, apparently lifeless, her head at an awkward angle.

"I thought you'd broken your neck for sure," she shuddered when she ran into her aunt's room a few hours afterward and found her in bed with a wet cloth upon her forehead. "We all did, in fact. I was quite frozen with horror, Joanna, when I saw you go. You seemed to fall forever. It was like a dream, you know, when you try to scream and can't; then all of a sudden I was screaming bloody murder and everybody was reining in the horses to see what had happened. It was horrible." Tears came into her eyes. "I just sat there, Joanna. I could not even dismount. I was too afraid of what I might discover. The whole thing continued like a nightmare and I was willing myself to wake up—as you do in dreams sometimes, you know—and it was only afterward that I recalled the strangest thing. Uncle Jack was the farthest away from you, for he was racing Rees and Felicia and was ahead of both of them."

"He would have been, of course," Joanna smiled involuntarily.

"But he wheeled his horse faster than you can imagine, then jumped off it and stumbled the last few steps, not even caring to be careful not to limp. By that time the other men were running toward you, too, but he made them all stand back."

"I guess he's quite accustomed to dealing with emergencies."

"So has Major Russell been, but Uncle Jack wouldn't let him near you. He ran his hand down your neck first and we could tell by his expression it wasn't broken. I tell you, Joanna, I had never

152

prayed so hard in my whole life as I did in those few seconds." Her eyes filled with tears again and Joanna smiled her gratitude. "Then Uncle Jack sort of straightened you all out, running his hands over your limbs too." She giggled here. "I don't think Felicia liked that part above half but he was most professional. And, oh yes, he pulled your skirt down." Joanna stared at her in horror and she giggled once again. "Don't look so shocked. It was only up a bit above your boot tops. You even manage to fall in a ladylike manner, don't you know. But he was most solicitous. He kept saying, 'Joanna, Joanna, wake up, Joanna,' ever so softly. I could hardly believe my ears. I never suspected Uncle Jack could be so tender. I was amazed. He really does care for you, Joanna. It was plain for everyone to see. Especially Felicia Pelham."

"I expect he forgot himself there for a moment," she replied. If so, he had not been the only one. Her face flamed at the recollection. But she had had some excuse. One could hardly be responsible for the actions one committed while partially concussed. Also the childish game they'd been playing when she fell must have contributed to her bewilderment. For time had done a turnaround. She was sixteen again and Jack was bending over her, his eyes concerned and tender, while he softly called her name. She remembered that with great effort she had opened her eyes in response. When she saw his troubled face, it was perfectly natural to reach up and touch it and smile her reassurance. "It's all right, Coppy," she had said. And then reality came flooding back.

"She seems to have joined the living most dramatically." Felicia's voice was acid. And Jack's face shuttered once again behind the usual mask he wore.

153

"Are you all right?" Toby asked, his voice quivering and then breaking into sobs.

"I'm fine, Toby," Joanna managed to reply, convincingly, she hoped. For she knew that the public tears were bound to mortify him. Godwin went over to stand next to the child and handed him a handerchief. "Why don't you ever carry one yourself, monster," he growled rather unsteadily, but the insult served to restore Toby's equilibrium a bit. Joanna tried to sit up then, which was a mistake. The world began to spin and she felt a warning wave of nausea.

"Lie still, Joanna," the major said. It was the first time she recalled his making free with her first name and it earned him a dirty look from Jack. Captain Rees was removing the cape he wore and spreading it on a patch of withered grass, a sacrifice Joanna would never have expected him to make and one which touched her deeply.

"Can you move her, do you think? I believe she's lying on a pile of stones."

Jack was still kneeling over her. He had already put his arms underneath her shoulders and her knees to try and pick her up when Major Russell murmured, "I think you'd better let me do that, old man."

If looks alone could kill, the major would have been stretched out cold beside Joanna. But he took the blast of Jack's impotent rage quite calmly, staring coolly back. In the end, Jack released her and stood up—with great difficulty actually—but the major knew better than to offer a hand to help. Instead he lifted Joanna with gentle ease and placed her upon the cloak. This time she did manage to sit erect, and the earth slowly began to right itself as well.

"Well, the Saracens definitely seem to have won

the day." Felicia was at her waspish worst. "None of the Carrothers seems at home on horseback. I had thought Godwin was the only novice rider. No one told me that Lady Welbourne was a learner too."

"Lady Welbourne is hardly responsible for her horse's stumbling," Jack growled, seeming happy to find a target for his pent-up spleen. "She is a very competent rider. I taught her years ago myself."

"Oh, well then," Felicia retorted. "That would make her unexceptional."

"It would indeed."

"And Godwin may have only just begun to ride," Toby interjected, "but he already does better at it than you do. He has a good bottom and is not at all cow-handed."

Joanna intervened quickly before a quarrel could erupt. "How is Star? I do hope she hasn't lamed herself." Her mare was picking at the dried grass contentedly, oblivious to her part in the recent upset.

"She's perfectly sound of wind and limb," Captain Rees assured her. "I checked her out almost as thoroughly as Sir John was checking you." This last was for Felicia's benefit, Joanna had no doubt. She might wish to avert a quarrel but Captain Rees was not so scrupulous. He was obviously bent on mischief. Joanna felt it time to stand. She did so, assisted by Major Russell. "Well, shall we go on now?" she said with attempted brightness. "Where shall we picnic? I do beg pardon for temporarily putting a damper on our outing."

"You'll do nothing of the sort," the major told her firmly. "If you think you can manage the ride, though, I shall escort you home, where I think you should call in the doctor. Just to be on the safe side, don't you know."

"Let's all go home," said Addie.

"Oh, no," Joanna protested. "Please don't let me spoil the day any more than I've done already."

"I quite agree." It was Miss Pelham who spoke, of course. "It would only add to Lady Welbourne's discomfort, I'm sure, for us all to make too much of such a minor incident. Since the gallant major has volunteered to be the martyr, I vote that the rest of us spend the day as planned."

No one else replied "Hear! Hear!" In fact, they all seemed rather taken aback at her choice of words. But Addie, at least, realized that Joanna would be made more miserable if they changed their plans because of her. "Come on then," she said abruptly. "I'm sure Joanna will be glad to see the last of us. Do take some laudanum for the headache when you get home, Joanna," she added, rightly interpreting her aunt's look of strain.

After watching the major assist Joanna upon her horse and being assured she would likely remain in the saddle all the way to Bath, the rest of the party mounted and continued on their way.

"But the outing was quite ruined," Addie later told her aunt. "We stopped by a stream to eat the picnic Felicia had provided. She had sent the servants on ahead to set it out and it was lovely but quite wasted under the circumstances. Uncle Jack was cross as a crippled bear, and Felicia seemed of two minds whether to quarrel with him over you again or to try out her famous flirts. But what she actually did was to wind up sulking. And Rees was no help at all." She laughed suddenly. "He seemed determined to rub salt into Felicia's wounds by praising you to the skies. What a perfect lady you were! How brave of you to offer to continue when you were obviously in pain! You could tell he was trying to make mischief. And when Felicia would not rise to the bait—though she fairly ground her teeth at everything he said—he switched to working on Jack's temper, which was obviously at the boiling point already. He began to sing Major Russell's praises too. It was obvious, he said, that the soldier was head over heels in love, and he'd bet a monkey you two would soon make a match of it. And when Jack still refused to comment, the captain called him on it. Would he care to place a wager against the possibility?"

"And what did Jack say?" Joanna hadn't planned to ask the question. It blurted out of its own accord.

"He growled that he had no desire to lose his blunt. For the captain was right, undoubtedly. You and the major were clearly meant for one another. It would be a case of Goody-Two-Shoes marrying Sir Gallahad.

"Of course that caused Felicia to laugh that silly, hysterical laugh of hers and say 'Goody-Two-Shoes! What a capital description of Lady Welbourne!' Then Toby got furious and had one of his famous tantrums. 'You and Uncle Jack are not to call Joanna names! I'll not allow it!' And he threw his cold pigeon pie all over her. She stood up screeching and called him a little wretch, then turned on me for just sitting there. 'Aren't you even going to reprimand him?'

"And I said of course I was, just give me time, and I turned on Toby quite severely. 'Toby,' I said, 'it was perfectly horrid of you to have thrown the cold pigeon pie at poor Miss Pelham. I love pigeon pie above all things. Why did you not choose the India pickle? I do not care for India pickle in the least.' "

"Addie, you did not!" Joanna gasped.

"Yes, I did. And Captain Rees and Godwin went into the whoops. And Felicia was livid, she was so angry. She jumped up and onto her horse and went dashing off at a speed that made our charge upon Sham Castle seem like a crawl."

"And what did Jack say?" Again Joanna had to ask the question.

Addie's grin faded and she looked a bit uncomfortable. "Uncle Jack? Oh, he didn't say a word," she answered. "He just mounted up too and tore off after her."

There seemed little more left to say then and they simply looked at one another for a bit. "Could I dampen that for you again?" Addie asked solicitously, indicating the cloth upon Joanna's forehead.

"Yes, please do," Joanna answered. For suddenly the headache seemed a great deal worse.

Chapter Fourteen

JOANNA WAS TOUCHED by the concern her family showed, but at the same time she wished they'd all go about their business and leave her to herself awhile. Her head ached dully, perhaps as much from the humiliation she felt over being catapulted from her horse in front of Felicia Pelham as from the actual impact. For comfort, she held on to the set-down Jack had given to Felicia on her behalf. But it didn't really alter the fact that she always managed to feel countrified and awkward in the sophisticated Londoner's presence. Falling off her horse was just a natural progression, she concluded, from being dowdy, dull, and tongue-tied.

Addie and Godwin had both come into her room separately, stayed awhile, and left. But Toby kept popping in and out upon every pretext. He seemed to need frequent reassurance that she was, indeed, all right. Joanna restrained herself from telling him that she needed sleep if she hoped to ever lose her headache. For it occurred to her that in spite of the fact that he was usually such a happy, energetic little boy, Toby was also bound to feel deep insecurity. He had, after all, lost both his parents. He now feared losing her. So she tried to treat all his inquiries about her health, his questions about the locations of his various prized possessions, and all his plans for outings in the future with utmost patience.

Jack, characteristically, was more forthright. "Can't you see that Joanna's hagridden, Toby? Don't jaw her to death, for God's sake." He was dressed for the theater, in new evening clothes with close-fitting, tapered trowsers. He looked even more distinguished, to Joanna's mind, in the simple black and white than he had in his gold-trimmed uniform. Certainly his hair seemed a brighter copper from the contrast.

"Joanna likes for me to talk to her," Toby answered him defiantly. "Don't you, Joanna?" The question was rhetorical and he plowed right on. "And she needs some company. I'm sure she's blue-deviled because the rest of you are going on to the theater without her—which I think is very shabby."

"I'm sure that she does not agree with you." Joanna really wished they'd get over this habit of discussing her as though she were not there. "Joanna doesn't want us to make such a to-do over the fact that her horse threw her. It's not the first time she's taken a spill and it won't be the last, I'm sure."

Joanna saw what Jack was doing and she gave him high marks for it. He showed more perception about Toby's fears than she would have expected of him. Toby, however, chose to misinterpret his comment about the ordinary nature of her fall.

"You're just as bad as that odious Miss Pelham, saying that Joanna don't ride well. She's a bang-up rider—for a girl, at least."

"Toby," his uncle sounded exasperated, "I was not trying to imply that Joanna is an incompetent horsewoman. I quite agree with your estimate of her skills. I was merely trying to point out that anyone—me, or even a Nonpareil like you—is subject to parting company with a galloping horse that stumbles.

"But since you yourself have brought up the subject of Miss Pelham, let me tell you that you are to seize the first opportunity and apologize for your brattish conduct toward her."

"I won't do it."

Joanna was startled by the similarity between the two. The tall, slim, hard-jawed man glared down like Zeus poised with thunderbolt, while the small, stocky, round-faced youngster glared back in kind. They were only uncle and nephew, she recalled, and physically they did not show even that much kinship. But when it came to butting heads with stubborn pride, few fathers and sons were more alike. Suddenly the incongruity of their toe-to-toe standoff struck her funny bone. The hero of Waterloo had met his match in a scruffy eight-year-old. She laughed.

Jack, to her surprise, answered with a rueful grin. "You're not helping, Joanna," he said. "The lad can't be allowed to get away with that sort of conduct."

She did her best to sober up. "Toby, he's right, you know," she said severely.

"He is not. Miss Pelham was a beast. She should apologize for all the shabby things she said. S-she didn't care at all that y-you might have been killed."

For a horrified moment Joanna feared he was going to cry again, a humiliation he would find hard to bear. Jack must have thought so, too, for he said quietly, "I don't dispute the fact you had some provocation, Toby, but even so, a gentleman does not throw pigeon pie upon a lady."

"Miss Pelham is not a lady. I heard Emma say so to Banks and he didn't question it."

Jack reverted to his former thunder-clouded stance. "You've no business eavesdropping or repeating servants' gossip."

"I wasn't eavesdropping. I just heard them talking. It's not my fault they don't like Miss Pelham. The thing is, you're the only one who does like her. Addie and Joanna don't like her. And Miss Newcomb's her aunt and even she don't like her above half. And Godwin used to be besotted and write her mushy poems and act a silly gudgeon, but I don't think he likes her either any more. So that makes you the only one. Except for Captain Rees," he amended thoughtfully, "and he's just about as ramshackle as Miss Pelham."

Jack was really angry now. "Whether you—or the rest of the family—like Miss Pelham or not has nothing to say to the matter. The point at issue is your ungentlemanly conduct."

"You ain't going to marry her, are you, Uncle Jack?"

"That is none of your damned business."

"It is my business if she comes to live with us. Which I should hate above all things. And it's Addie's business too. And Joanna's. Even Godwin's."

"If you think I'm going to take a poll about whom I marry, you are sadly mistaken," Jack retorted, then pulled himself short. "But I can see you're merely raising a dust to cloud the issue. I expect you to apologize to Miss Pelham at the first opportunity." He bade them an abrupt good night and left.

"I'll never apologize," Toby informed the door Jack closed behind him.

Toby also left to see the theater-goers off and to have his supper in the nursery. Joanna picked up Fanny Burney's *Camilla* that she had borrowed

162

from the lending library and tried to settle down to an evening of reading pleasure. But though the book had been recommended by Miss Newcomb as a most engrossing tale, she could not keep her mind upon it. Instead she kept hearing Jack declare how little he cared what the rest of them thought of Felicia Pelham. He'd marry to suit himself.

Someone knocked softly upon her door. When she called, "Come in," her abigail popped her head inside.

"I was afraid you might be asleep, ma'am," she explained the tentative tapping. "Mr. Banks says that Major Russell is downstairs and wonders if you are up to seeing him."

"Tell him I'll be right down," she said, glad to be distracted from the path her thoughts were taking.

"Are you certain, Miss Joanna?" Annie sounded disapproving. "Mr. Banks says that Sir John told Master Toby not to bother you, that Dr. Heyer said you needed rest."

"I'm feeling much more the thing," she said untruthfully. "Tell Major Russell I shall be with him shortly."

The major was looking rather conscience-stricken as Joanna walked into the small parlor a little later. "You look amazing well," he said with obvious relief as he removed his large frame from the dainty gilded chair he sat on and strode over to take her hand.

Joanna was wearing a puffed-sleeved spotted muslin dress of palest yellow that Annie, who seemed to approve wholeheartedly of Major Russell, had selected for her. The maid had also pleaded for time to arrange her mistress's hair properly in curls, but Joanna had bade her be con-

163

tent with brushing it softly back in a Grecian style. From the major's expression she judged that it, and she, met with his approval. "Did Banks lead you to believe I was at death's door?" she asked him.

"Yes," he grinned, "and that I was almost certain to shove you through."

"Well, it isn't so. I'm glad of company." She started for the delicate chair he had just vacated, thinking to preserve it, but he led her to the settee instead, then sat down beside her. "I was feeling quite abandoned," she said with a smile. "Everyone else has gone to the theater, I'm afraid."

"I know. That's why I insisted on Banks's finding out if you could see me. You're too popular by half, Joanna. It's almost impossible to be alone with you."

The way he was looking at her was rather disconcerting. "Let me ring for tea," she said.

"No, Joanna, please. No tea. No Toby. I really do need to talk to you."

She did not say, "Oh, what about?" or anything along those lines, for she thought she knew. And she despised coyness. She just sat there wishing she'd told Annie she wasn't up to seeing the major after all.

Her expression must have betrayed her, for the major studied her a bit and then said ruefully, "You're wishing me to the devil, aren't you, Joanna?"

"No, of course not. It's only that—that I'm not certain I'm ready just now for this conversation." She tried to smile at him to dull the sting her words might carry.

"You think I'm rushing my fences, do you? It's hard to swallow that, for you must have suspected from the first just how it is with me. It seems to have come to everyone else's attention, at any

164

rate," he said a bit grimly. "But I'm not asking you now what you feel for me. I think what I really want to know is how you feel about Jack Welbourne."

"About Jack?" She tried to treat the question lightly. "I hardly know how to answer that. Like a brother, I suppose. Of course we stay at daggers drawn far more than Godwin and I do—" Her voice trailed off at the sight of the major's face.

"Stop it, Joanna. That won't wash, you know. I saw the way you looked at him this morning when you came to and he was bending over you. My God, if you ever looked at me like that, I'd carry you off immediately."

"Oh, that."

"Yes, that." He smiled painfully. "I'll tell you honestly, Joanna, like every soldier I've been through a lot. But when the horse threw you and you lay there so still and pale, I thought that was the worst thing that could ever possibly happen to me. But I was wrong. It wasn't. The worst thing was when you smiled at Welbourne and reached up and touched his face."

Her own face grew hot at the memory. "It was a mistake," she said. "I was confused, you see. You knew—or at least I understood you to imply you knew," she was stumbling awkwardly over her words now, "that Jack and I at one time were very close. But then I married his cousin instead," she wound up miserably.

Major Russell did his best to help her. "Jack and I were close too on the Peninsula. Or at least I thought we were, though he wasn't one to open up to anybody actually. But he did mention once, when more than a little foxed, that he'd been jilted."

She flushed a bit at the word and he said, "Sorry. Anyhow, finally I realized from some things Toby said that you were the girl he had been in love with. But I kept hoping it was all past history. Until I saw the way you looked at him today."

"It is past history," Joanna said. "That was just a moment out of time, I think. I was totally confused. And he was there—and I thought for a bit that we were children once again. That's all."

"All," he echoed. "What do you intend to do about him, Joanna?"

"Do? There's no question of my doing anything where Jack's concerned. You must know how he feels about me."

"No, that I do not," he answered. "And I wish to God I did. It would make my lot easier."

"He despises me now. And I think he intends to wed Miss Pelham."

"I pray you're right. And I'd do anything in my power to bring it about—pay for a special license, hire a coach for Gretna Green, dance at the wedding—anything." He had tried to make a joke, but it fell flat. "Well, damn Jack Welbourne anyhow. What I really need to know is, do you think, in time, you could learn to love me?"

"I-I don't know, Major Russell. I really hadn't thought."

"Of course you've thought," he said impatiently. "It's not your style to be so missish. And you could at least drop the major and call me Charleton, don't you think?"

"Yes, of course. But—Charleton—I'm not trying to be missish, I'm truly not. It's just difficult to sort out all my feelings. So much has happened. Gerald's death," she stumbled over her husband's name and the major looked remorseful, "then Jack's return hasn't been easy for me. I can't pretend that there were not leftover feelings there."

"I'm sorry, Joanna. I really am. This was bad

timing on my part. But you see," he smiled wanly and suddenly she wished with all her heart that she could love him, "I am head over heels in love with you. I had planned to be very cool and level-headed about it all and make myself indispensable by degrees until one morning you'd awaken and re-alize 'I really can't make it without Charleton Russell in my life' and we'd be married and live happily ever after. What do you think, Joanna? Is such a thing impossible?"

"I don't know," she told him honestly. "I do like you very much."

"So does Toby."

"And that's no small recommendation," she said lightly, rising to her feet. "Couldn't we just leave it this way for a while?"

"I suppose we'll have to." He shrugged and stood up. "Except allow me one liberty. So at least you'll be able to separate my feelings for you from those for Toby." Then suddenly, and she realized after-ward, quite expertly, he pulled her into his arms and kissed her lingeringly. Though she did not give him much encouragement, she could not find it in her heart to break away.

"It seems I cannot walk into my own house these days without finding that damned dog upon my doorstep. Now there's a dog in the manger in my parlor."

Neither of them had heard Jack enter. They jumped like thieves caught in the till and sprang apart. He limped toward them, his blazing eyes fo-cused on Charleton Russell's face.

"What's the next step, Charlie? An offer of Carte Blanche? You'd best make it a handsome one. I've no need to remind you that my cousin is not one of your Portugese light-skirts."

With a strangled oath, Major Russell threw a

punch. Jack could not quite sidestep it and only partially blocked the blow that landed near his eye. He retaliated with a facer that sent the blood gushing from the major's nose while Joanna screamed and pulled frantically at the bell.

Charleton whipped out a snowy handkerchief and began to staunch his blood while Jack assumed a boxer's stance, breathing fire and brimstone.

"Put down your fives, Welbourne." The major spoke thickly through his handkerchief. "I can't fight a cripple and you damn well know it."

For a moment Joanna thought Jack would spring straight for the other's throat. He looked one slight step from murder. But he controlled himself enough to say, "The cripple seems to have the best of it so far, so the hell with your scruples."

"And the hell with your arrogance!" the major snapped. "Face facts for once. I know damn well that I could not have stood up to you before. But now you can't move well enough to feint me out. My first solid punch would mill you down."

"You're sure of that?" Jack snarled. "Let's put your theory to the test." But at that moment Banks came rushing in, followed closely by Jack's man. Joanna's shriek had outdone the bell, she realized.

"Will you bring some tea please, Banks?" was all she could think of to say.

"Tea! Don't be such a peagoose, Joanna," Jack said nastily as the major bristled. "Banks, fetch some brandy. And Dawson, you get a wet cloth for the major's nose."

As the servants left to perform their missions, looking nervously back over their shoulders as they went, Jack turned once more to Major Russell. "If you won't box me, how about pistols then? You can't claim that having only one leg will ruin my marksmanship."

168

"For God's sake, quit talking like an ass!" Major Russell was obviously at the end of his tether now, and Joanna could not blame him. "I'm not about to make a cake of myself—or a corpse either, damn your eyes—by standing up to you. There's no reason for it. Joanna's no schoolroom miss to need your chaperonage. You know damn well I was not insulting her. You can pretend to think I was offering Carte Blanche if it makes you happy, but as a matter of fact I was proposing marriage."

Jack turned a trifle pale. "Oh, and what answer did you get?"

"That's none of your damned business."

"Then, from the posture I caught you in, I surmise I should wish you happy."

"It would make a welcome change," Charleton retorted. "As far as I can discover, you've been wishing everyone to the devil ever since you lost your leg at Waterloo."

At that moment Banks and Dawson returned from completing their commissions. If Joanna hoped this would prevent Jack from replying, the hope soon died.

"I've heard this lecture before from your fiancée," he said. "I can see that you and Joanna have much in common. One of you is quite as prosy as the other." And he reached over and took the brandy decanter off the silver tray that Banks was holding. "I'll take this and bid you both good night. Joanna, why don't you wipe the blood off your hero's face?" He gave a mocking bow and left.

"Allow me, ma'am." Dawson was carrying a towel and basin. "There now, that's it," he said after a few moments of expert ministration. "The bleeding's stopped. But you'll have a bit of swelling I expect, sir." Joanna could not tell which observation accounted for the satisfaction in Jack's valet's voice as he picked up his basin and went out.

Major Russell walked over to the looking glass above the mantel and surveyed his countenance ruefully. "A bit of swelling," he said bitterly. "I'm going to look like a freak in half a minute. I may be able to forgive Welbourne for the facer," he added lightly for the servant's benefit, "but I'll not forgive him soon for making off with the decanter. Do you think you might rectify the situation, Banks?"

"Yes, sir. Right away, sir."

"And a glass of wine, please, for Lady Welbourne."

Later, when Banks had come and gone once more, Charleton raised his glass. "I'm sorry the brandy's only medicinal," he said. "I'd like to be toasting our betrothal. But I'll not abandon hope. And right now perhaps it's just as well. It's hard to be romantic with a swollen nose."

He was right of course, Joanna thought. To even speak of romance now seemed almost ludicrous.

Chapter Fifteen

JOANNA LAY AWAKE far into the night, her thoughts a jumble of confusion. She heard Addie and Godwin arrive home and go whispering down the hall. She smiled to herself in the darkness. Even in whispers they were bickering. The French clock on the mantelpiece struck two and later three before she heard Jack making his way none too quietly to bed. She could not tell whether his artificial leg or his degree of intoxication was hampering his progress, but when he lunged noisily against her wall, she decided she had best get up and see about him. Guided only by the dim glow of a streetlamp filtering through the window, she snatched up her dressing gown and flung it on, tying the ribbons as she ran.

Jack was slumped against the wall. His eyes were closed, no doubt to stop the world from reeling. "You've shot the cat good and properly," Joanna muttered, sounding more like Toby in her use of the cant phrase for drunkenness than like herself. Very carefully she removed the candle from his nerveless fingers. His eyes opened about halfway. "Is that you, Joanna?"

"Yes, it is. Come on to bed now. Are you able to walk?"

"Oh, yes," he answered thickly. "I can walk all right. They made me a brand-new leg and said,

'There now, Major Welbourne, you should be able to walk almost as good as new. You can't run any more, of course, or—or—play cricket, or go for long tramps through the woods, or dance, or—' By God, I did dance, though, didn't I, Joanna?"

"Yes, you did, Jack," she answered. "You were splendid."

"No, not really," he said disconsolately. "Felicia was. Not me. I was a fake. I didn't do a damned thing but stand there and hold her hand while she pretended to be on stage. She likes that sort of thing, you know."

"I know." If her tone was rather frosty, he took no notice.

"I can't dance any more and now Charlie won't fight with me because I'm a cripple and it would not be sporting. Charlie's very sporting, you know, Joanna."

"There's no need to say you can't fight any more," she said, trying to stop his maudlin self-pity and move him toward his bed, "for you bloodied Major Russell's nose quite shamelessly."

"I did, didn't I." He grinned. "And it was good for old prosy Charlie. Old Prosy has a bloody nosy! Old Prosy has a bloody nosy!" He snickered at his schoolboy humor but quickly grew morose again. "He was right, though, damn him. I couldn't have stood up to him for long. Footwork is most important in boxing, Joanna. Did you know that?"

"I have heard it." She put her arm around his waist and tried to tug him from the wall. "Put your arm on my shoulder, Jack, and I'll help you to your bed. Come on now, walk!"

Instead he pulled her into his arms. "Watch out for the candle," she yipped, trying unsuccessfully to stay at whisper level. "And come on to bed."

His shoulders began to shake and he looked

172

drunkenly down at her. "I ain't as foxed as you might think, Joanna. And I'm wondering what the *ton* would think if they could see sweet, proper Lady Welbourne in her nightclothes with her hair tumbling round her shoulders—and may I say that I've never seen you look more beautiful, Joanna, not even at the Upper Room in that rose-colored dress when you waltzed with Rees. But a woman always looks best dressed in her nightclothes and you're no exception, Joanna—" He broke off suddenly. "Do you know what else I can't do besides not walk so well?"

"You can walk, Jack, now come on," and she gave him a tug that got him started down the hall, leaning upon her heavily. But Joanna's success with his mobility did not distract his train of thought. "Can't run—can't box—can't dance—"

"Don't forget tightrope walking," she gasped as she strained to open the bedchamber door and staggered inside with him.

"It's cruel to make fun of a cripple," he said reproachfully while she managed to place the candle on the nightstand when they lurched past it. Heartened by this small success, Joanna tried to deposit Jack upon the bed. She more or less succeeded, but he dragged her down as well. She lay there for a moment panting from the exertion of practically carrying him while he still held on to her.

"Where was all that strength when you needed it to walk?" Joanna fumed as she tried to extricate herself.

"I can't walk—and I can't run—and I can't dance—and I can't box—" He was caught up once more in his drunken litany. "But do you know what else I can't do, Joanna?"

"No," she whispered fiercely, "and if you don't let

go of me I'll show you what else I can do—scream bloody murder!"

"I can't make love to a woman, that's what." There was real pain in his drunken voice.

"I know better," Joanna replied, trying once more to pull free of him. "I've seen you in action, remember?"

"Don't be so dense and missish, Joanna." He pulled her closer still till suddenly her shortness of breath could no longer be attributed to her exertions. "I mean I can't make love to a woman in bed like this."

"Well, thank God for it," she managed to say. "Now will you please let go of me?"

"It's not that I really can't," he went on thickly. "It's not a physical impossibility, you understand. But I just can't stand the thought of undressing and being seen like that. Do you know that I haven't had a woman since Waterloo, Joanna?"

"No, I didn't know," she answered, "but I'm sure it's done wonders for your character. Now let go of me."

"Character be damned," he snarled. "Morality's got nothing to say to anything. It's just that a woman would be repelled by a chopped-off stump —or pity it—or think it funny."

"That's ridiculous and you are maudlin drunk. Now will you let me go?"

"That's right—you've already seen my stump, haven't you, Joanna?"

"Yes, Jack, I've seen it. Now let me up."

"And you pitied me—don't deny it—it was there, written on your face."

"I was sorry it had happened," she retorted. "Who wouldn't be? Now let me up. But I don't pity you. I mostly want to wring your neck."

"That's true. I really don't think I'd mind undressing in front of you, Joanna. It wouldn't be the first time, would it? Remember when you were four and I was six?" He started to chuckle at the memory.

"No, I don't. And if you were a gentleman—"

"Joanna, would you care to stay and try it?"

"I would not," Joanna said, a lot more firmly than she was feeling.

"That's right. We mustn't do that, you and me. Old Charlie would not approve. And Gerald would go spinning in his grave—spinning and spinning and spinning and spinning—Joanna, I do believe I'm going to be sick." He suddenly let go of her.

"Don't you dare," she hissed, wondering whether to get the basin like a trooper or ring for Dawson like a coward. Cowardice was winning; then she feared there'd not be time. She ran and snatched the basin off the washstand, quickly dampening a cloth from the pitcher there. By the time she got back to the bedside, Jack was sound asleep.

Joanna managed to pull the covers from under him and tug off the boot from his good leg. But as she was removing his cravat, his eyes fluttered open once again. "Good night, Joanna," he said.

"Good night, Jack." He reached up and pulled her down and kissed her, as Toby might have done. Then he sighed, rolled over, and began to snore.

Joanna stood looking down at him for the longest time before she picked up the candle and went back to bed.

Not surprisingly, Jack's place at the breakfast table was empty next morning.

Five minutes after Godwin, Toby, and Joanna had seated themselves, Adelaide came breezing in. "It is the most perfect day for riding. You should have come with me, Godwin." She had been cantering down by the river with the daughter of one of Miss Newcomb's new acquaintances. "You'd have enjoyed it prodigiously now that you're a Nonesuch rider."

"I would not have," Godwin replied rudely through a mouthful of ham. He looked pleased nonetheless at her compliment. "For I'll bet a monkey that you and Miss Householder had every loose screw in Bath dangling after you."

Addie tossed her pretty head. "If you like to term Sir Giles Hough or Lord Exeter or Mr. Randolph Cranston loose screws, you may of course." She piled her plate full at the sideboard. Her recent social successes had banned all thoughts of weight reduction from her mind. "Not to mention Reggie Winfield." This young swain had attached himself to Addie to the extent of writing love poems to her—much to Godwin's ill-concealed disgust.

"He'd make a loose screw list, no mistake. As would Maximus Rees, who was no doubt among your entourage as well."

"Of course." Addie smiled at him provokingly. "By the way, Joanna," she turned to her aunt as she sat down, "what on earth went on last night?"

"Why, whatever do you mean?" What indeed! As Joanna's mind raced back over the previous evening, she grabbed her tea and gulped it, hoping its heat might account for a sudden flush at the thought that someone could have seen Jack and her sprawled out upon his bed.

"Uncle Jack was foxed as anything when Godwin and I got home. We saw the light in the library and thought we'd say good night. He nearly bit our heads off. What got him into such a taking? He was fine when he left the theater at the interval to take Miss Newcomb home. She wasn't feeling quite the

176

hing, you see, and he said he'd take her home and meet us afterward. I wish he had come back, for Captain Rees was going to take us to this place he knows of where they play faro. The lady conducts the most genteel evening right in her home, he says. All the *ton* go there and it's unexceptional. Felicia planned to go, of course. But Godwin got all high in the instep and said it would not be the thing for me." Joanna looked at her brother with no small respect while Addie glared at him. "If Uncle Jack had come he'd have taken me."

"I'll bet a monkey he wouldn't have," Godwin countered.

"And I'll bet another that he would."

"You'd lose then, Adelaide." Jack stood in the doorway on crutches. His trowser leg hung empty. He must be feeling a great deal of discomfort, Joanna realized, for of course he'd worn the artificial one all night.

Though freshly shaved and dressed immaculately, he definitely looked the worse for the past night's drinking bout. Joanna observed with secret pleasure some discoloration near his eye where Major Russell's fist had landed. He sat down at the table, laying his crutches on the floor beside him. Banks appeared at his elbow and poured some tea. "Allow me to fill your plate, sir." Jack blanched at the very thought. "Just a roll, perhaps. Good God, Addie, how can you?" He looked with loathing at the piled-up evidence of his niece's healthy appetite.

"I wasn't bosky last night, that's how," she answered. "But why wouldn't you have taken me to play faro?" she persisted.

"In the first place, I wouldn't have gone either because I have better ways to lose my blunt than by gambling with Jack Sharps."

177

"We could have gone and just watched the others. I daresay you would have gone there with Miss Pelham."

"Perhaps."

"Why is it, then, that you and Godwin admire her prodigiously because she flouts convention, but when I want to do any of those same things, you both are horrified?"

"Because for one thing she has cut her eyeteeth already and you have not."

Addie opened her mouth to retaliate but for once decided that discretion was indeed the better part of valor as she looked at her uncle's bloodshot eyes and haggard face. Instead she pushed her chair back and stood up. "I promised Miss Householder that I'd definitely bring you with me to the Pump Room," she said to Godwin. "To round out our loose screw list, I suppose," she added mischievously. "I'll just have to change into a walking dress. I won't be a moment." She skipped out of the room while Godwin excused himself and followed.

"You do look awful, Uncle Jack," observed Toby, who had been staring at his uncle ever since his entrance. Joanna tried to hide her smile behind her teacup. "Did you really shoot the cat last night?"

"Yes." Jack glared repressively.

It's unlikely, though, that Toby would have dropped the subject had not Banks appeared just then to say, "Major Russell is downstairs."

"By God, this is the outside of enough!" Jack exploded. "Does that fellow have to be always underfoot?" He glared. "After last night's episode I don't see how he has the gall to show up here. For God's sake, Joanna, can't you keep him at arm's length at least till we manage to have our breakfast?"

"Major Russell is not here to see me," Joanna answered mildly, trying to keep both Banks's presence

178

and the precarious state of Jack's health in mind. "He's taking Toby on an excursion."

"I'll go right now," Toby said diplomatically and jumped up from the table.

"No, you'll sit down and finish your breakfast first," Joanna said firmly. "Major Russell won't mind waiting a little longer."

"Of course not. The good major is all amiability." Jack's tone, unfortunately, reflected none of that same quality.

Toby looked at him curiously. "Uncle Jack," he said as he crammed the last bite of bacon into his mouth, "did Major Russell tell us a whisker when he said that you and he were friends?"

"Not exactly. I suppose we could have been considered so. We were comrades-in-arms, at any rate."

"I don't see why you don't like him now. I think he's a brick."

"I can see that," his uncle growled. "Joanna," he turned his bloodshot gaze her way, "you are, I hope, aware that I am Toby's guardian, not you."

"Of course." She looked at him warily, wondering what he had in mind. "Why do you ask?"

"I mean to point out that Russell's courtship of Toby is misplaced. He stays with me, no matter whom you marry."

Toby's fork clattered on the china plate as he let it go. He turned a white face toward her, his eyes large with apprehension. His lower lip quivered as he asked, "Are you going away, Joanna?"

"No, I am not," she answered firmly. "Your uncle Jack has the headache brought on by an excess of brandy—and let that be a lesson to you, by the way. Gentlemen do not overindulge in spirits. Consequently he is trying to be as disagreeable as he knows how. And I must say that he has learned to raise disagreeableness to new heights."

Joanna was now as furious at Jack as he was at the world. "Drink your milk, Toby," she said with authority; then not bothering to change her tone she turned on Jack. "And you might use the interval while he does so to go down and apologize to Major Russell for last night's disgraceful conduct."

"I damn well won't apologize."

Toby's wide eyes stared over the rim of his glass. "What did he do, Joanna?"

"I don't think I should discuss it."

"Was it really bad enough to apologize for?"

"It was, most assuredly."

"Well, Uncle Jack, aren't you going to?"

"No, I am not."

"Good. Then I guess that means that I don't have to apologize to Miss Pelham either."

There was a long silence while nephew and uncle stared at one another. "Checkmate," Jack said finally. "No, I guess you don't."

"Good." Toby jumped up. "But I'm sorry you and Major Russell are mad at one another, for he's taking me to Weston Village to see a steam carriage demonstration, and I do wish you'd come along. You'd like it above all things, I know. Couldn't you come with us anyway and just not speak to the major very much?"

"No, Toby, I could not."

"I thought not. Well, good-bye then. Good-bye, Joanna." And he stopped by his aunt's chair to let her hug him and kiss him on the cheek, a most un-Toby-like concession.

Joanna sat quietly until she heard the front door close. Then she unleashed the fury she'd been bottling up. "That was despicable of you—upsetting Toby like that. How could you!"

"He needs to know the truth. He will not go with you when you marry. So if that's your intention, you'd better start cutting his leading strings."

"I have no intention right now of any kind. But if I did have—and when I do need to cut the leading strings as you call it—I will attend to it myself and you may be sure it will not be done in such a cruel, tactless way." She was working herself up into a flaming passion.

Jack looked at her warily. "Ease up now. That's coming it a bit strong. Tactless, maybe. But certainly not cruel."

"It's cruel to frighten Toby about losing anyone he cares for. I've told you that before."

"It's a cruel world." Jack's hard eyes bored into her. "And the sooner he realizes it the better."

"Fustian. You aren't thinking of Toby's good at all. It's just that you despise me so much that you turn on anyone who is not in full agreement with you. It's one thing to lash out at Major Russell for that reason. He has many friends and can well afford to lose a fair-weather one like yourself." His eyes narrowed at the term. "But Toby is quite another matter. And I will not allow you to hurt him because of me."

"You won't allow it?" They were about to join battle on a royal scale and Joanna realized that she was actually looking forward to it. She couldn't say exactly when the change had come about—perhaps as late as last night when she had maneuvered him drunkenly to bed—but she had ceased to feel guilt where he was concerned. A hair shirt is too uncomfortable to wear forever, she supposed.

"You are in no position to tell me how to conduct myself," Jack answered furiously, but still remembering to keep his voice low enough to escape the servants' ears. "Especially where Toby is con-

cerned. He is my nephew, after all, not yours."
Then inexplicably his fury melted. "Goddamn it
all, you're right of course. I should not have said
what I did in front of him. It's just that I feel as
though someone's working my head over on an
anvil."

"Serves you right," Joanna replied.

He gave her a set-down look. "And you have a
valid point, I suppose, about my taking out my anger on all your bosom beaux."

"I'm glad you see that." She knew she should
have been more conciliatory now that he was showing signs of reasonableness, but Joanna was riding
a wave of anger such as she had seldom known.
"Anyone that has the slightest regard for me is
sure of your disapproval. I should not be at all surprised to learn that Miss Pelham's great attraction
for you is that she dislikes me almost as much as
you do."

His stare became icy once again. "I suggest that
we discuss Toby and not Miss Pelham. I admit I do
dislike seeing Russell win him over merely for your
sake."

"Charleton likes Toby," she retorted. Jack raised
his eyebrows, apparently at both the statement and
her use of the major's name. "Oh, I'm sure his interest is partly to please me," she conceded, "but
even so it's not 'merely for my sake' as you describe
it."

"No? I disagree. You dote on Toby and he sees
toadeating the boy as the best route to your affec-
tions. And I don't like it one damned bit."

"Well then, if you're jealous of Toby's friendship
with Charleton, why don't you spend some time
with him yourself? He idolizes you, you know. And
you are his uncle. Charleton cannot hope to compete with that."

"I have no desire to begin bear-leading eight-year-olds."

"That's your loss then."

He poured out more tea for himself, then as an afterthought refilled her cup. "You've changed, Joanna," he observed, not for the first time.

"We've all changed," she answered bitterly.

"True." He took a long and apparently restorative drink of tea. "Were you telling Toby the truth just now—about having no marriage plans I mean?"

"I wouldn't lie," she answered haughtily.

"Oh, no? Well, let that pass. I don't think you can keep Russell dangling forever, though. He may seem pliable, but he's actually very stubborn and usually gets what he wants in the long run."

"Major Russell must do as he sees fit. But I am not rushing into any marriage."

"That's very wise. You really should look around a bit more first. Oh, Charlie's a good fellow—in spite of all I've said and done, I'll hand him that. And I don't doubt that in many ways you'd suit."

"Like Goody-Two-Shoes and Sir Gallahad?"

"Good God! Does everything get repeated in this family? I apologize then for what I said. Besides, I'm not so sure it fits you. Charlie may be too nice for you at that."

"Thank you."

"Not at all. But I still advise you to wait a bit. His fortune isn't large, and with your ability to cause every male you meet to fall in love with you, you probably can do much better. Shop the Marriage Mart a bit more, Joanna, before making up your mind."

"I am not on the Marriage Mart," she retorted. "That was your idea entirely, to get me off your hands. But I don't have to remind you, surely, that I have already experienced the married state and am not at all desirous of embarking upon it once again."

"You sound bitter," he mocked. "Was not the title worth it?"

"Yes, I suppose it was." She gave him a level stare. "Not the title, but what went with it. Our marriage was what is politely termed one of convenience, you know. And Gerald and I both got what we'd bargained for. In my case, for one thing, my father's gambling debts were canceled. You know he'd lost most of what was left of Godwin's inheritance to Gerald."

"No, I didn't know. Well, well. If so, it was the first and last time Gerald was ever successful at cards. But then your father was a bigger fool than he was."

Joanna refused to take his bait. "And Gerald got what he wanted from the marriage too. Scoring over you pleased him more than any dowry."

"And so from that auspicious beginning you both lived happily ever after."

"No, that we did not. But as in most matches of the kind, we learned to accommodate ourselves in time. He formed interests elsewhere and came back to Welbourne Hall less and less. Our marriage was probably as successful as most of our class's are. But I won't deny I felt relieved when it ended." His brows went up again. "Yes, relieved. Quite guiltily, of course. But Gerald's death was an escape for me. And I'll not pretend otherwise. So you see, I'm not at all unhappy with my single state. And though I'm sorry to burden you, I don't wish to rush into another 'convenient' marriage."

"Russell's no Gerald."

"And Gerald wasn't the bogeyman you've made him out to be. He was mostly weak, which turned him into a bully. And he was completely selfish, of course."

He laughed dryly. "Is that your idea of a recommendation?"

"I'm merely trying to point out that his qualities weren't the stuff real villains are made of. If you had stayed around to become a bit more mature yourself, you'd have seen that."

"Since Gerald threw me out as soon as he reached his majority, I could hardly do that, could I? I will say this for him, though. He did buy me a commission. Gerald made damned sure I went as far away from him—and you—as possible. Chock full of brotherly love was our dear, departed Gerald," he finished bitterly.

"So were you. If the positions had been reversed, would you have wanted him around?"

"God no," he answered. "But I doubt I could have brought myself to kick him out. So Gerald wasn't quite as weak as you pretend. That took a bit of resolution."

"Perhaps he had more cause for jealousy than you."

"That's a joke. He had everything. Except you, of course. And he soon took care of that." Jack suddenly pulled himself up short. "How the hell we got off on this subject is beyond me. Having the devil's own splitting headache seems punishment enough for last night's debauchery without rousing all these sleeping dogs as well. So if you'll excuse me." He retrieved his crutches from where they lay beside the chair and hoisted himself up.

As Joanna watched him propel himself across the room, she asked, "By the way, Jack, have you told Miss Pelham yet about your leg?"

He turned and gave her an appraising stare. "As

185

a matter of fact, I have not. Not that it's any of your affair."

"It isn't, of course. Just idle curiosity, I suppose. I beg pardon for it."

"Speaking of curiosity, Joanna, I remember very little of what went on last night. After mine and Russell's spat, I mean. I was into the brandy pretty deep, I guess. So did I dream it, or did you actually put me into bed?"

"You did not dream it."

"Oh. Well then, just exactly what did happen?"

"Why, for one thing," she told the falsehood without the flicker of an eyelid, "you made me an offer of Carte Blanche."

His brows shot up. "I did? That was certainly reckless of me, considering the impecunious state I'm in. And what answer did you give me?"

"I fear I turned you down."

He looked at her searchingly, suspicious that she was roasting him, though not really sure. Then he gave her a mocking smile. "A pity that," he said.

Chapter Sixteen

THE NEXT FEW days passed uneventfully while Toby dinned the ears of his family in praise of the marvelous steam carriage he and the major had seen in Weston Village. "It looks just like a regular carriage, you understand," he told them solemnly, "except up front there are two small wheels and the coachman sits down low and turns them with a stick. The pipes for the steam are in the back and it all comes out in great huge clouds with the most marvelous hissing and banging you've ever heard."

"Doesn't it scare the horses?" Addie's mind had obviously been on other things.

"Of course not, you peagoose! That is quite the point. There are no horses."

"How odd," his sister answered. "It will not catch on. You may be sure."

"Toby." Jack put down the book he was reading to glare at his only nephew. They were spending a rare evening at home together and Banks had just removed the tea things. "If I take you with me to see a mill next Saturday, will you absolutely promise never under any circumstances to mention Richard Trevithick's infernal contraption again?"

"Oh, sir, do you really mean it?" Toby's eyes were as wide as the departed tea tray.

"A prize fight?" Joanna was horrified.

"Savage Sutton is fighting the Terrible Rudolf."

Jack's eyes remained on Toby while he studiously avoided hers. "They're setting up a ring a few miles out of town where there will be room to accommodate all the crowds and carriages. Would you like to go with me?"

"Oh, yes! I should like it above all things!" St. George in full armor standing on a dragon could not have held a candle to Toby's uncle.

"Jack Welbourne!" Joanna turned loose the full blast of her righteous indignation. "Of all the rackety, irresponsible suggestions I have ever heard, that one beats them all!"

He then had to look at her, his face all injured innocence. "What the devil are you rattling about, Joanna? Are you not the one who said Toby and I should spend some time together?"

"But a—boxing match!" She choked on the very words.

"Whyever not? Russell's covering all the educational things. It's up to me to see to it that the lad turns out well balanced. Of course you can forbid the expedition if you've a mind to." He gave her a wicked grin.

One glance at Toby's face was all Joanna needed to appreciate the full scope of Jack's Machiavellian maneuver. The horrified expression would have been appropriate had she threatened to push him over Dover Cliffs.

"You w-wouldn't forbid it, would you, Joanna?"

The look she shot at Jack spoke volumes and seemed to amuse him enormously. "As your uncle is fond of pointing out," she said to Toby, "he is your guardian, not I. But I really cannot see what there is to be enjoyed in the spectacle of two men savaging each other like mindless beasts."

"Oh, I say now, Joanna, it's not like that at all," Godwin chimed in to Toby's delight and her disgust.

188

"Savage beasts just don't apply. Boxing is a science."

"Why don't you come along then, Carrothers, and point that out to Toby," Jack said politely.

"Capital." Joanna's brother grinned. "I thought you'd never ask."

"Men!" Addie's face mirrored her aunt's distaste. Both women rose and fairly flounced from the withdrawing room. But no one seemed to notice their theatrical retreat. The talk had turned enthusiastically to the careers of the various "bruisers" past and present while they argued all the finer points involved in the art of fisticuffs.

If Joanna and Addie had thought to escape the boxing talk, they were much mistaken. Trevithick's steam engine was no more confined to a single track than was the male conversation in their part of the Royal Cresent. And if the previews of the mill seemed tedious, the reviews were far, far worse.

Toby, whose sense of the dramatic operated fulltilt on far less auspicious occasions than witnessing a fight, outdid himself in his account. His female relatives listened ad nauseum as he contrasted the cock-of-the-walk expression on the champion's face with the modest, manly demeanor of the Terrible Rudolf as he threw his hat into the ring. "But then they stripped," Toby informed them solemnly, "and when I saw the muscles the Terrible Rudolf sported, I knew that Savage Sutton was in grave trouble. And did I not say so, Uncle Jack?"

"Indeed you did, Toby. Several times in fact."

They had just finished eating a small nuncheon during this particular recital and Jack had lighted a cigar and was "blowing a cloud" while Toby entertained. The smoke was not thick enough, however, to conceal the gleam of amusement in Jack's eyes.

"Savage Sutton had it all his own way at first, isn't that so, Godwin?" Her brother grunted but Toby had not waited for his assent. "He flew at Rudolf like a tiger and milled him down in the very first round. Blood was gushing from his nose—"

"Toby!"

"Should I say 'gore,' Joanna?"

"You might talk of something else entirely."

"But you have to know what dire straits the Terrible Rudolf was in or you can't begin to appreciate his victory. At the end of the first round, no one would have predicted in a million years that he'd go on to draw the champion's cork. Even 'Erbert thought he was done for, and he's a real knowin' 'un when it comes to boxing."

Toby, by some miracle, as he described it, had spotted the small chimney sweep in the throngs surrounding the fight arena and they'd formed a fast friendship during the proceedings—which made one more score for Joanna to settle with his Uncle Jack. " 'Erbert said he'd bet a monkey that the Terrible Rudolf had had the breath beat out of 'im."

At that moment Banks mercifully appeared. "A note for your ladyship," he murmured as he extended a silver tray. Joanna recognized the major's handwriting and felt her cheeks grow hot under Jack's supercilious gaze. Toby stopped his recital to watch her read. "Who is the letter from, Joanna?" he inquired.

"That's none of your business, Toby," Addie reproved him sternly.

"Why? It is a secret?"

"It's from Major Russell," Jack informed him, blowing smoke rings nonchalantly.

"Is he coming over? I say, that's splendid. I can

190

tell him about the mill. When is he coming, Joanna?"

"He isn't coming here. He's asked me to join him and his mother at the Pump Room." She saw no reason to avoid Toby's question. Or to conceal the contents of the note from Jack.

"To meet Mrs. Russell—how cozy," the latter murmured. "A delightful lady, I understand. A bit caper-witted though. Russell usually keeps her under wraps." Joanna glared and he smiled back.

"Would you care to walk to the Pump Room with me, Addie?" Joanna asked, mostly to change the subject.

"I'd like to, Joanna, but Godwin and I have planned to walk to the Circulating Library." To her aunt's surprise, Addie appeared a little flustered.

"They have *Childe Harold* there and I particularly wished Adelaide to become acquainted with it," Godwin hastened to explain, turning slightly pink himself. "If you don't mind her not going with you this time," he added with untypical politeness.

"Oh, no, of course not."

"We could come to the Pump Room afterward, if you like and do the polite with Major Russell's mother."

"That would be nice."

"Well now, come along, brat." Godwin grinned at Toby. Their master-pupil relationship seemed to be much improved, Joanna thought. She decided she'd been wrong in condemning fisticuffs so heartily. For boxing did seem to make bosom beaux out of the noncombatants. "Let's see if you can last a full round with Caesar," her brother told his pupil, adding, "I'll meet you in the hall in an hour's time, Adelaide," and the three of them went out.

Joanna started to rise too, but she noted Jack's speculative gaze as he watched Addie and Godwin

191

smile shyly at one another over Toby's head. She decided to hold her ground.

"Well?" she challenged.

"Well what?" He stamped out his cigar on a French bone china saucer while Joanna flinched.

"You should furnish something more appropriate then," he said, noting her reaction. "But I do not think you wish to discuss my smoking habit."

"No, I do not. The thing is, I could not help but note your disapproval when you looked at Addie and Godwin just now."

"Then you noted a lot more than I was conscious of."

"I know he's not a brilliant match for her," Joanna plowed on. "But would it be so bad? They've known one another since they were children and should deal well enough together. You will not hold it too much against him that he's my brother?" The anxiety was strong in her voice. Although Godwin and she were too different to be very close, she loved her brother dearly and was most desirous of his happiness.

"I'm willing to overlook the accident of Godwin's birth that made him your brother," Jack said dryly. His sister-in-law gave him a searching look but could not tell from his face whether he was teasing or serious. "I'll admit though that I feel a bit uncomfortable even thinking of matching my niece with a man whose estates are all to pieces. It's enough to send my sister whirling in her grave. Arabella was quite ambitious, you may recall. But Addie does not have to marry money, thank God for that. So if she wants Godwin, I would not stop it. But don't you feel this conversation is rather premature? Where men are concerned Addie is fickle as they make them. I expect Godwin is simply her latest flirt. And he gets no high marks for con-

192

stancy. Addie may simply be salve for his wounds from 'Fair Felicia.' "

What Jack said made a great deal of sense. Still Joanna was not convinced. "You may be right. But somehow I do not think so."

"Time will tell, of course. But let me say it now, Joanna. I'll be true to my guardianship enough to see to it that they wait. Addie must make her come-out and Godwin finish school. Then if they still fancy themselves in love we'll talk of marriage."

"That's only sensible."

"Good God, you approve!" He stood up. "Let's terminate this conversation quickly before we revert to daggers drawn. Besides, I'm thoroughly sick of all this puppy love. May I escort you to the Pump Room to meet your aging swain?"

"Major Russell is about your own age, surely?"

"Of course. That's what I mean. True, he does not have my cares to turn him prematurely gray. Though he seems hell-bent on taking them over voluntarily. But then I always did see Charlie as something of a pompous fool."

Since she had no desire to fight with him so soon on the heels of his newly acquired reasonableness, Joanna contented herself with a speaking look as she left to change into a walking costume.

She took no small pains with her toilet, brushing her hair until it shone, then hiding most of the results with a brand-new high-crowned bonnet sporting an enormous ostrich feather that she felt made it all the crack. Whether she was taking so much trouble on Mrs. Russell's behalf or Jack's Joanna did not bother to consider. The answer could have made her most uncomfortable.

She did wonder, however, what had prompted Jack's sudden civility and his offer to escort her to the Pump Room. Perhaps he wished to hold out the olive branch to Major Russell. It was certainly time to curb his jealousy of his former friend. For even Joanna now realized it rose from the fact that some vestige of his old affection for her still remained. It had been there for all to see when she had fallen from her horse. And it had surfaced again upon the occasion of her putting him to bed. She sighed deeply at the recollection, for the insight brought no comfort. She could not always be knocking herself silly nor could Jack be forever drunk. And in the meantime she knew him well enough to realize that he'd marry Felicia Pelham in a minute rather than to admit his true feelings to himself. Nor would he bother to explore his reason for not wishing her to marry Major Russell. The sad truth was, Joanna had concluded, she might have married every day and every other man in Hampshire and he'd have forgiven her. But she had married Gerald and that put her quite beyond the pale.

"Joanna!" Her reverie was interrupted by Jack's imperious bellow from the bottom of the stairs. "Do come on before the damn Pump Room runs dry. Surely by now you'll pass Mrs. Russell's motherly inspection."

He looked her critically up and down as she came down the stairs. "Curse the luck. Since you've chosen to hide your face underneath that ludicrous-looking bonnet, I'd hoped you'd sprouted a huge wart on your nose or developed a squint at the very least, but no such luck. You're lovely as ever, damn Charlie's eyes."

"Thank you." Joanna looked at him suspiciously.

"For a woman of your age, I mean," he amended with a grin.

"Have you sent for invalid chairs?"

"No," he answered. "I plan to hop the entire way on one foot, leaning heavily upon your shoulder."

"In that case let's begin what must prove a very arduous journey."

He bowed mockingly and offered her his arm.

Chapter Seventeen

Joanna HAD FOUND few interiors so aesthetically pleasing as the Pump Room in Bath. Its classic proportions, dominated by huge Corinthian three-quarter columns but relieved from severity by its several alcoves, seemed to exude a quiet elegance while the statue of Beau Nash—who once was called the uncrowned King of Bath—gazed down upon the milling crowd from his recess above the Tompion clock like a patron saint, ever on the lookout lest someone should defile the hallowed halls by an act of social impropriety.

The room was, as usual, crowded when she and Jack arrived. People gathered dutifully to drink the healthful waters; but the more pressing reason was, of course, to see and to be seen—to pick up the various "on-dits" of Bath Society plus the London gossip delivered on the flying coaches that tooled down from the metropolis as often as three times a week.

As Jack and Joanna sank thankfully into chairs close to the warmth of a glowing fireplace, they were approached by Captain Rees, who looked as usual quite dandified in a pale pink coat, light gray pantaloons, and tassled black Hessians. And, as always, his shirt points were slightly higher, his neckcloth tied more intricately, his buttonhole a bit larger, than any other beau could boast. Joanna felt her understated, military escort flinch as the Corinthian came nearer.

"Well met," grinned Captain Rees, not unaware of the impression he was making. "May I join you?" Without awaiting their reply, he pulled up a chair. "Did not Miss Sadler accompany you?" he drawled. "I had longed most particularly to see her. I do admire her prodigiously, you know." He smiled languidly at Jack, but Joanna had the feeling he'd just thrown down a gauntlet.

Jack picked it up. "I know. And I cannot blame you. But I'm wondering if you are aware that my niece does not come into her fortune until she's twenty-five?"

Rees's eyebrows rose. "Twenty-five! What a perfectly Gothic arrangement."

"Yes, is it not? But somehow my family has always considered twenty-five to be a magic age. My cousin, for example, did not reach his majority till then."

"But surely—in the event of Miss Sadler's marriage?"

"Yes, as a matter of fact the age barrier to her inheritance could be overset then. Her father's will leaves that entirely to the discretion of her guardian."

"Which is you, of course." Joanna noticed that Captain Rees's smile no longer was reflected in his eyes.

"Just so."

"That *is* a bit of information worth mulling over."

"I thought you might find it so."

"You do realize, don't you, my dear Major Welbourne, that your news could force me to become your serious rival where Miss Pelham is concerned?" Rees smiled.

"The thought has crossed my mind. But then, have not you always been?"

To Joanna's relief this uncomfortable conversation was interrupted by the parties most in question. Addie and Godwin were approaching them, accompanied by Miss Pelham. Had Joanna not known that Addie and Godwin had set out together, she might have grouped them the other way around. For it was Miss Pelham who clung to her brother's arm and smiled flirtatiously up at him. She seemed to be at some pains to mend her fences where the poet was concerned. For what purpose Joanna could not imagine but suspected that Miss Pelham merely disliked having him slide so easily off her hook. What effect the lady's unleashed charms were having upon Godwin was not apparent, but it was most obvious that Addie's nose was out of joint. She sat down between her aunt and Jack, putting the greatest distance possible between herself and Godwin.

As the poet placed her chair, Miss Pelham nodded to Joanna in a manner that most charitably could be described as barely civil. She smiled winningly at Jack and Captain Rees. "I cannot begin to say how delighted I am to see you both. I have just been boring Mr. Carrothers to tears—now, Godwin, you were bored, you cannot deny it." She twinkled up at Joanna's brother, who turned beet-red under Addie's stony stare. "I have been prosing on and on over a pair of grays I've just purchased from George Chamberlayne."

"Chamberlayne sold his grays?" Rees was obviously impressed. "I don't believe it. Phil Starke has been trying to buy them for these three months, and George would not even discuss the matter with him. What on earth possessed him?"

"He was all to pieces, naturally. Done in by faro,

so he told me. At any rate, he was most anxious to part with them. And at a price that should have hurt my conscience."

"But will not, nonetheless," Rees interposed.

"How well you understand me," she murmured flirtatiously, then shifted her attention. "Oh, Jack, have you ever seen them?"

"No, I've not been so fortunate. But George spent at least an hour the other night droning on forever about what prime bits of blood they are."

"And he did not exaggerate. Why, they make the cattle we picked out for Maximus seem fit merely for pulling plows."

"Oh, come now," both gentlemen said together.

"It's true," Felicia crowed. "Those chestnuts can't begin to compare to my new grays. But there's no need to argue when I can easily prove my point. What would you say to a curricle race, Maximus? With a wager thrown in to make it more interesting?"

"Who would drive your team?"

"Need you ask? I would, of course."

"Well then, I accept the challenge," Rees retorted. "I'm willing to conceded that Chamberlayne's team could have the edge on mine—though to say there's no comparison between my pair and his is coming it a bit strong. But if you're to drive—well, that puts matters in a new light altogether. For my superior, and may I say 'natural' male talent should more than compensate for any inferiority of my cattle."

"Why, of all the odious, arrogant!—" Miss Pelham bristled, or pretended to. She turned again to Jack. "Surely, Sir John, you are not going to allow Maximus to malign me in such manner? Speak up for me."

Jack smiled down at her. "In this instance I cannot. For Maximus and I are quite in agreement. But if you like, I will volunteer to drive for you."

"I would not like it! What an infamous suggestion! You are as odious as he with your male superiority. Driving skill is the issue here, not brute strength—the only department in which I will grant men their superiority. But since we do not intend to pull our curricles ourselves, strength is not a consideration. And when it comes to brains and dexterity, or any other quality needed in a race, I consider myself more than the equal of any man!" She tossed her short curls and her eyes flashed indignantly. She looked magnificent. The men grinned at her indulgently while Addie and Joanna tried unsuccessfully to wipe their faces free of the jealousy that raged within them.

There was a great deal of discussion about a time and place. "Let's not dilly-dally," Miss Pelham said. "For I do not want the word to reach my prosy aunt. She would immediately send a servant up to London to fetch my father." She darted a quick look at Joanna, whose expression mirrored her dislike of hearing her old friend Miss Newcomb described as prosy. But Miss Pelham chose to misinterpret. "La me," she laughed. "I fear I've shocked poor Lady Welbourne. Did you ever see such disapproval?" She twinkled up at Jack. "Do make her promise not to breathe a word to my Aunt Newcomb. Or all the fun will be spoiled for sure."

"I am no tale bearer," Joanna answered for him.

"No? I am most relieved to hear it. Jack has said that you are quite a high stickler when it comes to duty."

"I hope he may be right." Joanna shot him a dirty look. "But that need be no concern of yours. I'm sure I feel no obligation where you're concerned."

"I do believe that our sweet Lady Welbourne has

just delivered you a telling set-down," Captain Rees chimed in. "So may we consider the matter settled then, Felicia? Tomorrow—ten o'clock—the London road?"

She complied and the two of them soon took their leave to go and drive the course in Miss Pelham's rig, to "get the lay of the land," as Captain Rees expressed it and to allow him to size up the opposition. "Go home and decide what family jewels you can afford to pawn," was his parting advice to Addie and Joanna. "You must not miss the chance to lay a sizable wager on the race. The smart money will be on me, of course."

"Of all the brazen, ramshackle, care-for-nothings!" Addie exploded once the pair had gone.

Surely you are not castigating Captain Rees?" Jack mocked. "I thought you were a great admirer of that Nonesuch."

"It's not Captain Rees I speak of and you well know it. It's that—that—hoydenish Felicia Pelham that you and Godwin make such cakes of yourselves over."

"Cakes? Oh, surely not," Jack drawled.

"Perfect cakes! I think it's shabby the way you encourage and admire her most scandalous behavior. If I were to suggest such a race you'd—you'd—"

"Lock you in the tower?" her uncle prompted helpfully.

"Exactly. Or something equally as odious since we don't actually have a tower. But you think Miss Pelham is a Nonpareil."

"I don't," Godwin said abruptly.

"You do, too. If you could have seen the moon-calf expression on your face as she kept batting her odious eyelashes up at you. I don't mind telling you I found it perfectly disgusting."

201

"Moon calf! I did not look like a moon calf. I couldn't have."

"Children," Jack interposed, "Major Russell's mother is bearing down upon us with Charlie in her wake. You can either stop your squabbling now or beat a hasty retreat and resume it elsewhere."

"Let's go," said Addie, jumping to her feet while Godwin followed.

"A wise decision," her uncle said. But to Joanna's vexation, he made no move to follow their example.

"Don't bother wishing me to Jericho, Joanna," he murmured. "I plan to stick by you like a brother. I must not have the dowager think your family has no interest in your welfare."

"My welfare!" she hissed underneath her breath. "You're only interested in making me feel as awkward as possible and you well know it."

She need not have worried, though. There was no chance to feel awkward around Mrs. Russell. That lady seized the conversation by the throat and began to worry it along the lines of her own invalidish condition and the failing health of all around her. As to the former, she looked robust enough, with round apple cheeks and bright brown eyes. She was short and dreadfully overweight, all in all a contrast to her son, which set Joanna wondering about the physical attributes of the late lamented Mr. Russell.

Introductions had scarcely been accomplished before the major's mother congratulated the others upon taking the waters while still young. "I myself have begun a course of them, following my doctor's order. I have sinking spells, you know. I am finding the treatment more efficacious. Are you liverish, young man?"

Jack looked understandably startled. "I think not," he answered while Joanna snickered.

"I cannot recommend the waters enough for preventing such a sad occurrence," she pronounced. "Have you had your glass today?"

"No, ma'am," Jack replied. "Indeed I never realized that people actually drank the nasty stuff."

Mrs. Russell contrived to look both shocked and pained. "It's easy to take one's health for granted when one is young and blessed." She sighed, her purple turban, one hue brighter than her purple walking dress, shaking solemnly on her head. "But one never knows when the hand of Providence may suddenly strike one down. Take my son, for instance."

They both looked at Major Russell, who turned beet-red to match his smitten nose.

"He will not like my calling attention to the fact, but you cannot have failed to note that the poor boy's nose is much enlarged and also quite inflamed. Liver!" she finished triumphantly.

Joanna gasped and Jack's shoulders began to shake. "You must certainly try the waters, Russell," he said, grinning at the major. "Your mother's right. That nose is bound to be the result of an ailing liver."

"And may I suggest that you yourself might benefit from holding your head underneath those waters for several minutes?"

"Why, Charleton, that's quite absurd," Mrs. Russell frowned. "If he followed your advice, the poor young man would drown himself. One must drink the waters for them to be of any benefit. Now will you please fetch some for all of us?"

"Certainly, Mother," the major answered dutifully, rising to his feet. "But first, will you accompany me in a turn about the room, Joanna?"

"Of course," she answered, giving Jack a mischievous look as she excused herself. She and the major then left to join the other strollers who were combining exercise with the advantages of seeing and being seen.

"Leaving Welbourne to deal alone with Mother should be ample vengeance for the pain he's given me." Major Russell smiled down at Joanna as he gingerly touched his tender nose.

"For shame. Your mother is quite delightful."

"Thank you for saying so. She is rather a dear, actually. Her heart is quite as enlarged as the rest of her. But my filial loyalty doesn't blind me to the fact that she is a nonstop talker. Especially on the subject of her ailments, which are legion, I might add."

Joanna glanced back to see that Mrs. Russell was indeed prattling at a rapid clip while Jack paid her surprisingly close attention. He must be finding her quite a rarity, she thought, for he was seldom polite enough to suffer fools that gladly. Her thoughts were interrupted when the major spied an old acquaintance whom he wished to make known to her. They talked a bit, or the men did at any rate; then Joanna and the major excused themselves to fetch the waters.

By the time they returned, Jack was looking quite glassy-eyed and stony-faced. His previous good humor and his amusement at Mrs. Russell's absurdities seemed to have deserted him. He refused the glass of mineral water proffered him.

"But you must drink it, dear Sir John," Mrs. Russell wailed. "It is so beneficial."

"Not to people with limited imaginations like myself," he replied curtly while Joanna felt her cheeks flame at such flagrant incivility. "If you will excuse me. Mrs. Russell, Joanna, Major." With the stiffest and slightest of bows he turned abruptly and left.

"What a strange young man!" Mrs. Russell exclaimed as her son and Joanna sat down on either side of her. "He was ever so charming at first and then he turned quite starchy, don't you know, and hardly said a word. His moodiness stems from liver. That's the only explanation. I know that I myself can be enjoying the best of health one minute— dear Charleton here will bear me out—and then find myself quite all to pieces in the next. Oh, dear me—I had not noticed!"

They followed her appalled gaze to where Jack was just going out the dark oak double doors. "Why, the poor young man is limping. There. You see. I knew it! He is liverish. He most certainly should have stayed to drink the waters."

Chapter Eighteen

WHATEVER BROUGHT ON Jack's sullen mood had not abated the next morning when Joanna passed him in the doorway on her way to breakfast. He replied to her civil greeting with an icy stare, and when she inquired whether or not he intended going to the "celebrated curricle race," he advised her nastily not to burden herself with his affairs. "You must have more important concerns weighing on your mind," he added, brushing past.

"Goodness—what was all that in aid of?" she inquired of the rest of the family assembled at the table.

"I cannot imagine," Addie answered, buttering her toast. "But he's been like a bear again this morning. He fairly snapped my head off when all I did was ask him—twice—to pass the marmalade."

"I expect he has the headache from drinking blue ruin all last night," Toby proffered his own theory. It occurred to Joanna that Toby had grown entirely too worldly wise of late. Jack's presence had benefited his nephew in many ways but it had also had its liabilities.

The talk turned to the curricle race taking place at ten. Godwin reported that news of it had spread like wildfire, and the whole of Bath promised to attend. "Having a woman participant is shocking without a doubt," he said, for Addie's benefit,

Joanna guessed, "but it is also quite a drawing card. The tipsters are having a field day, I'm told. Almost as many wagers are being placed on this event as on the Rudolf-Sutton fight."

"I suppose most are backing Captain Rees." Addie's nonchalance was not deceptive.

"As a matter of fact," Godwin looked uncomfortable, "most are betting on Miss Pelham. Chamberlayne's horses are the better pair, you know."

Addie sniffed. "I for one shall put my money on Captain Rees. He is the far superior driver. Whom do you intend to back?" she challenged.

"I never wager, can't afford to, don't you know," the poet answered diplomatically, if not truthfully.

"Toby, would you like to go with Major Russell and myself?" Joanna asked to switch the subject. "He'll be bringing his gig around. I've asked Cook to prepare a picnic for us."

"Huzzah!" Toby waved his spoon on high. "I should like it. I had planned to—" His voice trailed off.

"You had planned to sneak out of the house and hare it over there on foot," Godwin finished for him. "Admit it, brat."

"All right. But this will be much jollier."

Addie and Godwin had already laid plans to attend the race with a group of their particular friends. Jack's plans remained a mystery. His family speculated that he'd left the house early to join Felicia. "If she had the least bit of gumption, she'd let him drive the race for her," Addie sniffed. "But she'll dote on the attention with no regard for her reputation or for the fools that risk their money by betting on her." This last was a direct jibe at Godwin and, from the way his face turned red, Joanna suspected she had caught him out.

If, a short time later, Major Russell was none too

pleased to have Toby along in a chaperon capacity, he was much too kind to allow the lad to know it. The three of them traveled to the race site in an open phaeton with Toby ready to man the hood if the low-lying clouds suddenly opened up, as they threatened to do at any moment.

The major and Toby filled the time with a technical discussion of the various points of the competing horseflesh and a disparaging assessment of women drivers. Joanna was of two minds about the latter. Her feminity made her long to launch into a spirited defense of her own sex, but her antipathy toward Miss Pelham bade her hold her tongue. As she saw the major grinning down at her, she realized he quite appreciated the horns of her dilemma and had been baiting her all along. "You odious man," she muttered and he laughed.

The starting point of the race was thronged with carriages and spectators when they arrived. The racers had chosen a straight stretch of road that sloped downhill, giving the best view possible for the crowd and an easy getaway for the competing teams. The audience, Joanna surmised from the description she had listened to ad nauseum, was the same kind of throng that gathered for the fights, with this exception—there must have been at least as many women present as men, due no doubt to the sexist nature of the contest. But, as with the boxing matches, the audience was a cross-section of society. Nabobs brushed elbows with the scum, and every trade and calling was represented. "Watch your reticule," the major muttered as he tooled his gig skillfully into a meadow overrun with wheeled conveyances of every kind from carts to coaches, with people seated in, around, and on the tops of all of them. "There's probably a pickpocket to be found for every dozen of us."

"Oh, I say, there's 'Erbert." Toby let out a whoop. "Halloo there, 'Erbert!" Joanna saw the dirty little chimney sweep who was elbowing his way skillfully through the crowd break into a broad grin and wave.

"Speak of the devil—" the major muttered and Toby turned to glare indignantly.

" 'Erbert is not a pickpocket," he declared. "You don't even know him!"

"I do beg pardon. You are right, of course. One should not generalize.

"We'll do best, I think, to remain here where we are," the major observed after looking the area over carefully. "We should be able to see over the heads of most. Toby, stand up on the seat if you'd like."

"Oh, I say—there's Addie and Godwin," Toby reported from his vantage point, "way over there across the road down in the next field. They can't see nearly so well as we can," he concluded with satisfaction after vainly waving for their attention.

Captain Rees was already at the starting point, lounging nonchalantly against his curricle while a groom fussed anxiously about. "I didn't know that Captain Rees is a member of the famous Whip Club!" Joanna exclaimed, feeling suddenly more secure of the small wager she had placed upon him as she took in every detail of the captain's sartorial magnificence. He was wearing an ankle-length, drab-colored coat adorned with huge mother-of-pearl buttons and four tiers of pockets. Beneath it shone a brightly colored, broad-striped waistcoat. His corded silk plush breeches had strings and rosettes at the knees and were tucked into short

209

boots finished with broad straps which hung over their tops all the way down to the Dandy's ankles. A broad-brimmed, short-crowned hat sat at a rakish angle on his Brutus crop. In a word, where the world of racing was concerned, Captain Rees was all the crack.

"I hate to disillusion you," Major Russell had also been drinking in every detail of the beau's attire, "but Rees is not a member of the Whip Club."

"But he's wearing their special livery."

"No, not quite," the major chuckled. "They could almost, but not quite, take him to task for counterfeiting. If you look closely you will see that his greatcoat sports four tiers of pockets, while the club's is only three. And his waistcoat stripes are green and yellow, not the blue and yellow of the Whips. No, I'm afraid his Whip Club membership is fully as spurious as his captaincy."

At that moment the crowd let out a shout and Felicia's rig came tooling into sight. The sun broke through the clouds a bit as she skillfully lined her team up next to Rees. The sun would shine forth for her, Joanna thought as she squinted skyward. She fully expected an orchestra to appear and break into the Hallelujah Chorus in Felicia's honor; that was the sort of sensation Miss Pelham always seemed to make.

Of course Jack was perched up on the seat beside her. "Plan to race me yourself, old boy? This is a wise move on your part, Miss Pelham," Rees called out loudly, much to the tittering amusement of the crowd.

"Indeed, he will do no such thing," Felicia retorted. "I plan to have the victory all to myself."

There was much laughing and catcalling and joking among the spectators as the starters and judges of the event discussed the rules with the participants. They were to drive a ten-mile circuit, it had been decided, and judges—and spectators too, no doubt—were stationed all along the route to make certain that nothing untoward would happen.

"Are the drivers set?" one of the officials called out loudly as Jack dismounted after apparently wishing Felicia luck.

"Not quite," the captain drawled. "It occurs to me, Miss Pelham, that this all seems rather flat without a wager."

"You surprise me," she called back. "I personally have already placed some blunt upon myself."

The crowd roared its approval.

"Oh, money," the Dandy shrugged. "Never having formed the habit of having any, I've never learned to value it. I was thinking of something more to my liking."

"Oh?" Miss Pelham eyed her friend suspiciously.

"I was thinking more along these lines—that if you should lose, my dear Miss Pelham—and of course you're bound to—" a burst of applause arose from the men, "then you shall give up carriage racing and marry me."

The crowd gasped while Miss Pelham looked speculatively at Captain Rees.

"And if I win? As of course I'm bound to."

He shrugged. "Then you get my curricle and pair."

She laughed mockingly. "That's hardly a sporting wager. Especially since I'll be most amazed if your rig is even paid for." Rees bowed his acknowledgment of the hit. "I know," Miss Pelham brightened up. "Since I seem to have staked my reputation on this venture anyhow, how would this be? If I lose, I wed you. But if I win," there was a pause while

211

the Beauty turned her gaze upon Jack Welbourne, "if I win, I wed Sir John."

Afterward Joanna tried to remember just how it went from there. The whole thing should have been hazy, for she felt as though she'd again been sent hurtling off into space over a horse's head, only this time there'd be no getting up and walking away.

She was sure, too, that the whole world held its breath. She felt the major beside her stiffen, and Toby clutched her arm tightly. The silence seemed interminable. "So what do you say, Jack? Is it a wager?" Felicia called out gaily, though Joanna thought the Beauty's voice trembled just a bit.

"Why not?" Jack's voice was loud and clear and certainly rock-steady, though Joanna wished it otherwise. "If Rees wins, you marry him. If you win, it's wedding bells for us."

The crowd went wild, sending up huzzahs that made the horses prance, giving both drivers all they could do to hold their teams in check. "Please let her be dumped and break her neck." Toby's muttering sounded strangely like a prayer and she almost said amen.

"They can't hold 'em any longer," someone called out to the starter, who obligingly fired his pistol into the air. "They're off!" the rabble shouted and the two teams exploded down the road, flying hub to hub, sending up a shower of spray as they parted the leftover puddles from an early morning downpour. As they ran neck and neck around a curve, the crowd cheered them out of sight, then settled back to await the final drama of their return, spreading cloths and pulling out the picnic lunches they had brought. The carriage trade mostly ate high and dry in or on their various vehi-

cles while the less fortunate made do with the still-
damp meadow ground.

"Shall we eat?" the major asked. "It will be some
time."

No one answered him, but he took up their basket anyhow and began to distribute the victuals it
contained. "This will help to pass the time," he
said. "I should not expect to see them for close to
three quarters of an hour."

"C-Captain Rees is bound to win." Toby's voice
was as unlike its usual self as was his appetite.

"He's quite certain to." The major's tone was just
a shade too hearty. Joanna could not appreciate his
attempt to reassure them, for she knew he must be
pulling for Felicia all the way. Or perhaps, she decided, he was merely indifferent to the outcome.
For he made great inroads into the cold chicken
and apple tart that neither Toby nor she could
touch.

After an interminable interval during which Joanna died several deaths, someone shouted, "Hark
now—they're coming!" and sure enough the sound of
racing carriage wheels could be heard around the
bend. The crowd held its collective breath. Then
one lone curricle swept into sight. The watchers
identified the horses first. They were gray, not
chestnut. And then they saw the woman at the
reins.

Felicia had parted with her hat somewhere along
the route and now perspiration caused her hair to
curl tightly around her head. The effect was like a
Roman frieze, the triumphant charioteer ready for
the crown of laurels. She slowed her team expertly
and pulled them to a stop precisely at the finish
line. As her groom leaped to snatch the horses' bri-
dles, she flung the reins down and threw her arms

up in victory while the crowd let out a roar. Still Rees did not come.

"Where's the captain?" someone shouted when the cheers died down.

"Back there in a ditch somewhere," she laughed. "Chivalry is not dead in England. I bluffed him out as we ran side by side on a narrow stretch. He took the ditch himself rather than pitch me into it."

"You cheated then!" Toby shouted out his rage, but if Felicia heard she gave no sign. Instead she jumped triumphantly down from the curricle into Jack Welbourne's outstretched arms.

Toby cried openly, and Joanna was hard put not to follow suit. The major made an effort to take them home at once, but there was no getting out of the jam of carriages just then so they were forced to sit and watch while the rabble milled around Felicia and her fiancé offering their congratulations.

After a bit, Rees came driving in. Some Good Samaritan had hauled him from the ditch and set his rig to rights. He congratulated Felicia with all his usual good-humored aplomb; then spying Major Russell's carriage in the crowd, he ambled over. He took in every detail of Toby's tear-stained face before he spoke. "Now here's a lad after my own heart," he said. "Where did we go wrong when it's only children who are allowed to show their feelings? Come on, Toby, ride back into town with me. I need your tears."

"I am not crying," Toby sniffed.

"Very well then. I need your fortitude. At any rate, keep me company."

Toby obediently climbed down and took the vanquished Dandy's hand and they set off across the field toward Rees's rig. Joanna longed to tell the boy to stay—that she also needed him, that she did not want Major Russell to reopen the subject of their marriage, even though there was no longer any reason not to speak of it.

Chapter Nineteen

JOANNA HAD NOT given the major credit for his tact. They drove home in silence interrupted only occasionally by some trivial comment on his part. He left her at the door saying gently that he would call on her in a day or so.

She sought the immediate comfort of her room but found none there. She could only sit and stare at the cold fireplace and think of Jack, finally and irrevocably wed to someone else. Though nothing had really changed, she thought. Jack had been lost to her for years. But she had neglected to extinguish the hope she held; now Felicia Pelham had finally destroyed it.

Toby stopped by her room a moment to say that he was home. Joanna had thought he'd wish to stay by her for comfort, but instead he announced that he was starved and went to raid the kitchen. "Would you like me to ask the maid to fetch you something?" he called back as an afterthought. She refused his offer, marveling at the resiliency of children.

Her mind raced feverishly. The trip to Gretna Green would take place at once. Of that there could be no doubt. Even Felicia Pelham could not face down the double scandal of her curricle race and her public proposal to Jack Welbourne. The two must be wed immediately.

216

Joanna toyed with the idea of going to Miss New-comb and telling her the story, but she realized the absurdity of such a plan. The gossipmongers would already have made a beeline to her door. And even if it were possible to send a message to Felicia's father in time to stop the Gretna Green elopement, Miss Newcomb would not wish to do so. Marriage to Jack was the only way to salvage her niece's character. The sooner the wedding took place the better, would be her attitude.

And so Joanna schemed all sorts of absurd schemes to stop the match herself. First, she considered telling Felicia of Jack's affliction. But as little as she thought of the other woman, she could not believe it would make a difference. That Felicia loved him, Joanna had no doubt. Next, she considered sneaking into Jack's room while he bathed and packed and hiding his artificial limb. How she would accomplish this under Dawson's eagle eye or how long a delay such an absurd theft would win, she could not imagine. At last she settled on a less dramatic but equally as hopeless course. She would try to persuade Jack not to go through with the marriage to Felicia.

She listened intently for his return. But as the afternoon wore on and he did not come, she went to Dawson to inquire of him. "Sir John sent round a note for me to pack his things and send them to Miss Newcomb's." Dawson was stony-faced. If he knew why his master planned a trip—and of course he did; servants always knew everything—he gave no sign. And if Joanna imagined he also disapproved, perhaps it was merely a projection of her own feelings onto his.

Again she sought the haven of her room. She lay on the bed till darkness fell. When the maid tapped on her door to inquire when dinner should be served,

217

she told her not to bother. Addie and Godwin would not be in and Toby could have a tray. As for herself, she had the headache and did not feel like eating.

"Master Toby isn't here, ma'am," the maid informed her.

"I expect he's just gone to Major Russell's to take Wellington for a walk," Joanna said. "He often does, you know." She would have to scold him later on, she supposed, for not getting permission before he left. But somehow none of it seemed to matter now.

Not long afterward the maid was back once more. "Captain Rees has called and asks to see you. Shall I have Mr. Banks say you're indisposed?"

"No, I shall be right down."

Joanna didn't bother analyzing why she agreed to see Maximus despite the fact that her head was throbbing miserably. Perhaps she welcomed any interruption to her thoughts. Or perhaps she viewed them both as fellow sufferers. For in spite of the captain's flagrant fortune hunting, Joanna had never believed that his feelings for Miss Pelham were all mercenary. His glum features when she joined him in the small saloon confirmed her impression.

"I've come to commiserate with you." He smiled wryly as he rose to his feet when she approved. "Somehow I couldn't face being alone right now or with any of my cronies either. Do you mind?"

"No, I'm very glad to see you." And she was. Surprisingly so, in fact. "Will you take a glass of wine?"

"The whole cellar, if you like."

Unconsciously Joanna was expecting Rees to pour out his soul to her, but then she realized that it was not the Dandy's style. He turned instead to the smallest of small talk. The closest he came to discussing the real reason that they were sitting there was to remark ruefully on the humiliation of being beaten in the race. "She knew me, damn it all. She knew I could not drive against her in the same way I would race a man. She let me lead, then came abreast just before we hit the narrow stretch. I tried to bluff her out, but she wouldn't pull her horses. She knew damn well I would not force her into the ditch. I should have done, however. And let her break her lovely neck."

"You certainly should have," Joanna replied solemnly. The wine on an empty stomach was having its effect. They both laughed at her heartless statement.

There were other evidences of her intemperance. She vaguely realized that her headache had all but disappeared. She also became fuzzily aware of some sort of commotion going on in the downstairs entryway. For some time the muffled but authoritative tones of Banks had seemed to dominate, but suddenly a child's voice rose to reverberating pitch. "I means to see the gentry cove, so lemme go!"

"Goodness—surely that's not Toby!" Joanna looked at the captain in some alarm.

"If it is, you'd best have his accent seen to immediately." He rose and walked out into the corridor with Joanna following close behind. At the foot of the stairs the little chimney sweep struggled to free himself from the grasp Banks had upon his collar. "Lemme go! I got to speak to the guv'nor," he shrieked. "It's life or death, I been telling you." The sight of the captain and Joanna may have given the urchin added strength. Or else Banks was too concerned with the effect of the sweep's grimy collar upon his white gloves for him to grasp it properly. But for whatever reason, the little boy wriggled himself free and came bounding up the stairs. "Tell that leery cove to keep his fives to hisself and off of me," he squeaked. "I ain't meaning to split to nobody but Toby's uncle."

The captain reached to clasp 'Erbert by the arm, but like the butler he was given pause by the filthiness of the sleeve that covered it. "Come in here," he gestured toward the parlor, "and tell us what you've come for. Toby's uncle is out of town, but this lady is his guardian and I'm a friend. Now what is all this uproar in aid of?"

Joanna felt herself grow cold sober with apprehension before the words were out. "It's Toby, guv'nor," the little sweep replied as Rees closed the parlor door behind them. "The gypsies snaffled 'im."

"What the devil do you mean?" the captain snapped and took a step toward 'Erbert who misinterpreted anxiety for menace and dodged behind a chair.

"Don't frighten him, Maximus," Joanna cried.

"No, don't be frightened, lad. Just tell us calmly what this is all about."

"It's about gypsies, that's wat it's about. They snatched Toby. And they're taking 'im up north."

The captain eyed the child suspiciously. "Is this some sort of Banbury Tale? How would you come to know a thing like that?"

"Because they brung 'im to me old man," the child retorted. "They means to sell 'im for a sweep, you see. So they tried me father first, so they wouldn't 'ave to lug Toby any further than they 'ad to."

"That's daft," the captain said. "No kidnapper would be fool enough to try and dispose of a victim on his very doorstep."

"That's wat me old man told 'em," the sweep answered solemnly. "Said 'e'd as soon 'ave the cathedral bells ringin' changes out his window as to have some local gentry-cove's brat sweeping our Bath chimleys. It was the gin, o' course. They'd been swillin' or they'd of knowd better all the time." The little boy was beginning to enjoy the drama of his tale. "Me old man put a flea in their ears and told 'em to take the boy up north. And that's where they've headed. And so I nipped out the window and come to tell you. Because Toby's by way of being me friend, you see," he finished proudly.

"Oh, dear God," Joanna said weakly.

"Lady Welbourne, don't you dare to faint!"

"I wouldn't dream of anything so missish. I'll be all right. But oh God, Maximus, Toby!"

"Steady now. How long have they been gone, lad?"

But the little sweep seemed to have no sense of time. The gypsies had come before dark. He was sure of that. But then he'd had to wait until his father was senseless with gin before he could make good his own escape. "Still—that's probably not much over an hour's head start," Rees mused. "And with the sort of horse cart affairs they usually drive they can't have gotten far."

"Jack!" Joanna said.

"I beg your pardon?"

"Can we overtake Jack, do you think? He'll know what to do. He'll get Toby back, I know he will. He l-loves the boy, you know."

"By Jove, why not? It's worth a try at least. Come on. My rig's outside. Thank God the whole world seems to be traveling in the same direction. I'll bet a monkey that we overtake Welbourne before we do the gypsies though. Somehow I don't see him as an overeager bridegroom. If he springs his horses, it will come as a surprise to me." The captain was actually grinning at the prospect of a chase. If he seemed lost to all proper feelings about Toby's peril,

221

Joanna could at least applaud his decisiveness. Thank heavens he was here, she breathed in gratitude. Then pausing only to snatch a cloak and to instruct Banks to feed the little sweep and reward him handsomely, she ran out into the night with Captain Rees.

All trace of the morning clouds had disappeared and the moon shone full and brightly. "A perfect night for kidnappings and elopements," the captain muttered as he did indeed spring his own matched pair. They headed out at a rapid clip.

After they'd covered a mile or more at breakneck speed, Joanna cautioned Rees about his horses. "After all," she reminded him, "they've already run one race today."

"Just half a race, you may recall." He grinned at her. "Besides, there's a posting house up ahead where I can change cattle if I need to, but I'm gambling it won't be necessary." They dashed on in silence for a while, the captain breaking it only once to advise Joanna to pull her hood up around her ears. Until then she'd scarcely noticed the chilliness. Then, just as she was thinking they must rest the horses before they dropped, "Ah—" the captain breathed and she saw the dim outline of a carriage in the distance. "It's Felicia and Welbourne, I'll stake my life upon it," he crowed, giving his tired team another flick of his driving whip. "I was right. He certainly isn't pushing his cattle to make good time. But he could not even if he wished to. She's insisted upon bringing a coach full of boxes stuffed with clothes. You won't catch our modish Miss Pelham making off in nothing but her shift.'"

And with a burst of speed that Joanna feared would be his team's undoing, they overtook the carriage as the captain noisily hallooed the coachman. That worthy pulled his vehicle to a shaky stop, convinced that he was being overtaken by highway-men.

"What the devil!" The coach door flung open and Jack stepped out, closely followed by Felicia Pelham.

"Maximus, what's the meaning of this!" She fairly shook with outrage.

"Oh, Jack," Joanna interrupted before Captain Rees could answer. "It's Toby. He's been k-kid-napped." Then to her horror she burst into tears.

"Fustian!" she heard the Beauty say.

"No, I'm afraid it isn't." Rees sounded so casual as to be almost languid. " 'Struth, old fellow. A little chimney sweep chap came round to your house to report it. Some gypsies picked the lad up. Foxed, you know. The gypsies, not Toby, naturally. And they tried to sell him to the sweep brat's father. He put a flea in their ears and told 'em to take their wares up north. Anyhow, we've set out in hot pur-suit. But Joanna felt we should appraise you of the situation first."

"I'm sure she did just that." Miss Pelham's tone was icy. At least it had the force of stopping Joanna's tears.

"What will you do, Jack?" she asked.

"He will continue on with me," the bride replied. "If anything has happened to Toby, which I'm much inclined to doubt, I'm sure Maximus can cope. Can you not, Maximus?"

"And you don't care a fig one way or another what happens to Toby, do you?" Joanna had traded weeping for seeing red.

"I care about continuing this journey. We are to be married. Not that I think you've forgotten that fact for a single moment."

"You can get married any time!" Joanna wanted

to scratch and claw and might have done so, too, had Rees's hand not fastened firmly on her arm. "But right now all that matters is that Toby is in mortal danger. Jack, what do you intend to do about it?"

"Go after him, of course." Jack's calmness made Joanna sound all the more hysterical.

"Don't do it, Jack. Can't you see this is merely a ploy to stop our elopement? She's in love with you, you know."

"What if I am? What has that to say to anything? It's Toby's danger we're concerned with. He's the only thing that m-matters." Joanna started to cry again. Before Felicia. She could have sunk.

"She's right, you know, Felicia. And you're wrong about this being some ruse that Joanna has manufactured. She's a lot of things, but she's no actress."

"And you are not stopping your elopement, just postponing it," Joanna interposed, trying belatedly to be more diplomatic.

"Here Welbourne, take my rig," Rees cut the conversation short and spurred them into action. "You and Joanna get going now. I'll escort Miss Pelham back to the Royal Crescent."

"You will do no such thing. I shall go with Jack."

"I think not. Lady Welbourne's ready to fly up into the boughs at the mere thought of not going after Toby. And the curricle ain't built for three. Besides, the boy can't bear the sight of you, you know.

"Now, as I was saying, Welbourne, Felicia and I will await you at the Crescent. And as soon as the boy's recovered, it's on to Gretna Green for you and her. No one need even know of the delay. But, and I should not have to point this out, right now we're wasting time. The longer we argue, the farther away the gypsies go. Oh, Claud—" he called up to Felicia's coachman who had been watching them

224

pop-eyed, "how far would you say we are from the next public house?"

"Not over two mile, sir."

"Good. Let's go there first, Felicia. I'm in sore need of a restorative. Also I've not eaten a bite since I lost that damned race and that's a fact. After that, we'll head back to the Royal Crescent. Good luck." He smiled benignly at the other two. "Take heart, Joanna, the lad will be all right," and he practically shoved the fuming Felicia into the coach. "Spring 'em, Claud," he called and they took off as Jack handed Joanna back up into the curricle.

"His team looks done in," he observed.

"It is," she answered. "Captain Rees says we can change horses just up ahead."

But Jack was expertly turning the team in the middle of the road.

"What are you doing?"

"Heading back to Bath, of course."

"What on earth! Did you not hear us say that they're taking Toby north?"

"North covers a deuced lot of territory. I'd like a word with 'Erbert's father before we ride off at random inquiring about the countryside for wandering gypsies."

"But his father will be of no use. He is intoxicated."

"We'll just have to sober him up then, won't we?" She looked on the verge of apoplexy, and Jack seemed amused. "Don't overset yourself, Joanna. We'll get the boy. It's only prudent to go home first and get my rig. Besides—every good hound has to sniff the rabbit first, you know."

"Toby is not a rabbit."

"True. But has it not struck you that there are several peculiar aspects to his disappearance?"

225

"Whatever do you mean?" she said impatiently. While she realized that the horses were done in, it did seem that he was coddling them beyond all reason. "Could we not walk faster?" she asked sarcastically.

"Not really. As I was saying, it surprises me that Rees didn't take time to talk to Herbert's father."

"He no doubt thought it a waste of time—a consideration you seem determined to ignore—and we needed to be off if we were to have a hope of catching you."

"That's another peculiar thing. Why did you come haring after me instead of fetching the able-bodied Major Russell?"

"Of all the heartless—selfish—odious—" she sputtered. "We came for you because Toby is your nephew."

"True. But Russell is your fiancé."

"He is no such thing!"

Jack stared at her. His face looked grim in the white moonlight. "Spare me your Banbury Tales, Joanna. Mrs. Russell told me of your engagement."

"She did what? When? Are you foxed yourself?"

"Not a bit of it. There in the Pump Room. She prosed on for fifteen minutes trying to decide whether you'd be married in the Abbey or St. Swithin's Church. She thought you preferred St. Swithin's."

"She had absolutely no basis in fact for such a statement! I don't mean about St. Swithin's but that I'm to marry Charleton. She must have let her imagination run away with her. I expect that Charleton had said he wished to marry me. And like any proud mother, she could not consider the possibility of my saying no."

"And did you?"

226

"Yes. Well—actually I said I did not wish to discuss the matter."

"Oh, my God! That shatterbrained old dowager! Is that the truth, Joanna? You are not engaged to Russell?"

"Certainly it's the truth," she blazed at him. "When did I ever lie to you?"

"The first time I can recall was when you said you'd elope with me. The second was more recent—when you told me I'd offered you Carte Blanche. I did no such thing, though when you kissed me good night so sweetly I was tempted for a bit."

Joanna looked up at him in horror. "You remembered!"

"Of course."

"What do you mean, of course? You led me to believe you were foxed out of all recognition."

"No, just foxed. I rarely get past recognition."

"Of all the—" She could only sputter. "Do whip up those beasts a bit."

"No. I've no intention of doing them an injury. The little difference in speed we could get out of them won't help Toby's cause. Climb down off your high ropes."

"I am not on high ropes."

"No?" They drove in silence for a bit. Jack broke it. "Was it true what you said to Felicia back there?"

"What exactly do you mean? And why the sudden inclination to consider me a blatant liar? That was never part of your low opinion of me before."

"Joanna, endeavor to behave rationally. I know it's been a trying day and you've reason to be overwrought, but don't take exception to every word I say. I want to know if it was true when you told Felicia you were in love with me." He forestalled her expostulation. "Or rather, to be more accurate,

227

when she accused you of being in love with me and you more or less admitted it. Is it true?"

He was looking down at her intently. She started to look away, feeling suddenly quite humiliated, but then she refused to be outfaced. "I don't think it's at all gentlemanly of you to bring the matter up and throw it in my teeth, for my agitation over Toby should offer me some excuse. But I'll not be missish. Of course I'm in love with you. That's never exactly been a secret," she added bitterly. "So if you wish to gloat over the fact during your wedding journey, I suppose I owe you that much and I wish you joy of it."

They rode in silence the rest of the way back into Bath. Jack guided the team toward a run-down neighborhood on the outskirts of the town and, after making inquiries of a passerby, pulled up in front of a little shack. "Wait here," he said as he clambered down. Joanna ignored the command and jumped down to follow him up a weed-filled path to the front door of the hovel.

Herbert himself answered Jack's fierce pounding. He opened the door only a crack, however. "Is your father home?" Jack asked.

"N-no, sir. He's down at the Rat Pit."

"How convenient." Firmly, although gently, Jack pushed Herbert and the door aside. "Toby!" he shouted. "Come on out now. The charade is over."

Chapter Twenty

IT WAS A very chastened Toby who huddled against Joanna on the carriage seat, trying to shrink into insignificance. "Oh, Toby, how could you!" she wailed, but Jack stopped her scold before it could begin.

"Stow it, Joanna. I don't think that frightening you to death was ever part of Toby's plan."

She hushed. They were almost home before the silence was broken once again. Then Toby piped in a very small-boy voice, "Where is Miss Pelham?"

"She's with Captain Rees," Joanna answered. "He's bringing her to the Royal Crescent. They should be there by now."

"T-then Uncle Jack still means to marry her?"

"Yes, Toby," she said gently. "Nothing has changed." He began to cry.

Joanna was thankful to observe as they approached the house that Rees and Felicia had not yet arrived. At least Toby would be spared the added embarrassment of their presence. For unless she could quickly concoct some Banbury Tale to cover him—and her mind set feverishly but barrenly to work—it would be obvious to them that Toby had staged his own kidnapping to foil his uncle's elopement plans.

"How about some supper?" Jack asked Toby as

229

they stepped inside the hall where all the servants gathered beaming their relief.

"I'm not hungry."

"Then, let's get you scrubbed down some and into bed," and so saying Jack stooped and picked up his eight-year-old nephew and flung him across his shoulder. Toby clung to him tearfully as Jack limped up the stairs.

It was some little time before Jack joined Joanna in the parlor—long enough for her to have gone from teary-eyed over the touching scene that she'd just witnessed to boiling mad. As he walked in and sprawled upon a wing-backed chair, she wheeled upon him in fury.

"This is a fine time for you to grow paternal!"

" 'Avuncular' I think is the more precise description."

"Whatever. The point remains it's ironical you should begin to show affection for Toby now."

"Not in the least. You must have observed how much I've mellowed since I've been home. I do believe I could even face Gerald with equanimity if he should—God forbid—suddenly rise up from the tomb. So it's not so wonderful that I should show affection for lovable little Toby. And I'd think you'd be pleased instead of flying off into the boughs."

"I might be, except that it comes a trifle late— just as you plan to abandon him."

"I've no intention of abandoning Toby. I made that clear to you some time ago."

"I don't care what you intend. He hates Felicia. He'll run away. Don't do it, Jack."

"Do what?"

"Marry Felicia, of course."

"Because of Toby?"

"Why else?" But Joanna felt her face turn red.

"Think of what you're asking me," Jack drawled.

"Of course never having been jilted yourself, you can have no idea of what it's like. My case is different though. I could never bring myself to behave in such a caddish manner."

She was stopped from replying by a tap upon the door. "Oh, God, they're here," she moaned.

"I think not. We'd have heard the carriage." And sure enough, Banks entered bearing a note upon his silver tray. "A groom from York House brought this for you, sir," he said.

Joanna sat with her eyes glued upon Jack's face as he read the message, but his expression betrayed nothing of its contents. "No answer seems required," he said; then, "Oh, Banks," he called to the butler's retreating back, "bring us some port, will you please?" He handed Joanna the note. "It seems I've been jilted once again."

The letter was from Captain Rees. Joanna had some trouble at first decoding the hasty scrawl. "Dear Sir John," it read,

By the time this arrives we should be well on our way to the border, and you will have realized that it was my intention all along, with Toby's inspired cooperation, to abduct Miss Pelham.

I expect some opposition on her part at first but am quite prepared to deal with it. I learned my lesson during the curricle race and have no intention of ever again allowing chivalry to get in the way of winning. Besides, after she recovers from her initial fury, I think the whole thing will appeal to her overblown sense of the romantic.

You've been a formidable rival, I must say, with your damnable good looks, hero's image, and missing leg. So she'll feel cheated at first, of course. But I think she'll come to realize in time that you two never could have dealt together. She would have loathed rusticating in Hampshire. And you'd hate London life. Besides, I shall appreciate her fortune far more than you ever could.

Give my best to Joanna. Tell her I admire her prodigiously. What a pity she is not rich.

Your obedient servant,
Rees

Joanna put the letter down and stared at Jack as Banks placed the wine decanter by his elbow and went out. He was still expressionless. "Felicia knew all along about your leg," was all she could think to say.

"So it would seem."

"I told you it would make no difference."

"You apparently were right."

"Do you mind?"

"That she knew about my leg? No, not at all. I've grown most insensitive. I may publish an account of my amputation in the London *Times*."

"You know I don't mean that. Do you mind that Rees has run off with Miss Pelham?"

Jack handed her a glass of port before he spoke. "Mind? About as much as Marie Antoinette would have minded, I suppose, if the guillotine blade had suddenly stuck about halfway down."

"Thank God," Joanna breathed.

She really didn't need the wine. She was already intoxicated. But she took a fair-sized gulp anyhow for she would not risk her Dutch courage suddenly forsaking her.

"Then would you care to go to Gretna Green with me?"

232

"Whatever for? Rees will see to it that we don't catch them. And I've just said I've no desire to."

"Don't play games, Jack. I'm asking you to elope with me to Gretna Green. Will you do so?"

"Good God, no."

The wine had failed her. Joanna's euphoria vanished as fast as it had come. She sat her glass down carefully and stood up. "Well, that's that then. I thought you had finally forgiven me. And I'd have a second chance. But I can see that I'm to be left at the head of the stairs once more."

Jack stood too. "Are you feverish, Joanna? You're here. In the gold parlor."

"You may be, but I'm back home in Blackthorn. At the top of those d-damned stairs in the dream I've been having ever since that night. You're down there at the bottom calling me to come away with you in spite of Mother and Father and Godwin and Gerald, and in my dream I finally find the courage and start toward you. Then I wake up and it's too late. Perhaps now I can finally face that fact. It's seven years too late. And I've just waked up once again."

"Go back to sleep then and keep on coming," Jack replied. "For God's sake, Joanna, don't stop now. You entirely mistake the matter. I only said that I do not wish to go to Gretna Green. Sight unseen, I loathe the place. I'm sick of the very sound of it. I can only hope I never have to go there. Let alone be wed there. Especially along with Felicia and Maximus. That was really a ramshackle idea, Joanna. Much better that we marry back in Hampshire with Toby and Addie and Godwin cheering us on and all our neighbors and retainers there nodding their heads and saying, 'It's jolly well time don't you think so?'"

"Y-you mean you do wish to marry me after all?"

"Try me and see. You can damn well keep on coming toward me. I think you owe me that much balm for injured pride."

She went. Straight into his arms. He kissed her and the room went spinning. "Don't keep me standing here," he murmured in her ear after a rather breathless interval. "I'm a poor hopeless cripple after all," and he pulled her down upon the striped settee that never before, Joanna would have wagered, had been put to such a use. After a long, long while Jack simply held her tenderly with her face snuggled against his coat of superfine.

"It's not at all as I've remembered it," she murmured.

"What's that supposed to mean?"

"Just that everything has changed, and we're two entirely different people."

"Good lord, Joanna. Don't tell me that after all that we've been through—not to mention your recent abandoned participation in our lovemaking—that you're about to decide it's all a big mistake."

She held him fiercely. "You know better," she declared. "I'm just trying to say we're starting over. We're two whole new people."

"You're whole. I'm merely new."

"You know what I mean. We are not children any more. And I love you as a woman, not a girl. More than I could have ever imagined. And you feel the same way too, so don't deny it."

"I wouldn't even try," and his mouth pressed hard against hers once again.

"Oh, I say, Addie! Godwin! Come quick and see!" Toby's voice piped excitedly as Joanna leaped up from Jack's arms like a triggered spring. Their family was gathered in the doorway staring at them openmouthed.

Jack laughed and pulled her back down again beside him. "Don't be so missish, Joanna. You've just said that we aren't children any more."

"Does this mean you're not going to wed Miss Pelham? Did mine and Captain Rees's scheme work after all?"

"Like a charm, Toby. Let me congratulate you upon your cunning. The Iron Duke himself could learn strategy from you. No, I'm not going to marry Miss Pelham. In point of fact, your Aunt Joanna has just offered for me and I've come up to scratch."

"Did you really propose to him, Joanna?" Adelaide looked impressed but rather shocked.

"Doesn't everyone?" Godwin asked in a *sotto voce* aside.

"She did indeed propose," Jack said to Addie, pretending not to hear Joanna's brother. "And I've no intention of ever letting her forget the fact. We'll be married back home in Hampshire. As soon as possible. You must all be there. To give the bride away."

"You aren't bamming us, are you, sir? No, you would not behave so shabbily. Oh, I say. That really is capital, Uncle Jack!" Toby rushed over to hug them both. "Of course I shall be there. Wild horses could not keep me from it. For I shall like your wedding above all things!"

There was something decidedly peculiar about
Lady Pickering's new maid.

AN UNCIVIL SERVANT
by
Marian Devon

Clearly, her lovely hands had never done a day's work. And when
Lord Jeremy Pickering kissed her in a fit of pique—promptly accepting a bucketful of suds in return—the apology he received after her
anger quelled was in words as aristocratic as his own. Catherine, obviously, was no maid. She was, in truth, a runaway bride. So a better
disguise was devised by her employer, the ever-helpful, rather eccentric Lady Lavinia Pickering, and under her wing Catherine became
the fourth member of a club devoted to adventure and intellectual
stimulation. As the foursome arrived in Bath, there was plenty of
intrigue afoot. For not only was Catherine's husband closing in, but
Lord Jeremy, too, had his sights set upon fair Catherine, determined
to save her virtue…and steal her heart!

Published by Fawcett Books.
Available in your local bookstore.